ULTIMA THULE

BOOK ONE

THE PALE LADY

Stephen Hernandez

Book Layout © 2017 BookDesignTemplates.com

Map illustration: Land of Dreams by Sydney Sime

Ultima Thule. Book One: The Pale Lady by Stephen Hernandez. 1st ed.

ISBN no: 978-1-9161126-7-4

For Linda Almond—the best of the best of friends.

"The one you trust most can disappoint you most."

—Fijotsdale Saga, c. 23

CONTENTS

1. INTO THE MAELSTROM 7

2. THE BEACH   9

3. THE JOURNEY   26

4. THE SEVEN DWARFS   33

5. THEDRAGON   44

6. THE ASGARDIANS   55

7. THE PALE LADY   58

8. LOKI'S REVENGE   63

9. THE CASTLE   71

10. LOKI AND THE DWARFS   77

11. SIF'S HAIR   83

12. EXCALIBUR   87

13. THE BUILDER   93

14. MERLIN   103

15. THOR AND LOKI'S RIVALRY   111

16. THE NUMB CITY   124

17. THE PLAIN OF FLYING DREAMS   130

18. THE WATERFALL OF OLD SONGS   143

19. THE MAN WITH NO NAME   148

CHAPTER ONE

INTO THE MAELSTROM

The Vikings were in deep discussion. The fog had lifted, and they were in a quandary because there was no sign of their fleet. They had been blown many miles off course and the thick fog, which had lasted many days, had further served to disorient them. They had waited until nightfall so that their captain and also chief navigator, Balder the Belly, so-named because of his enormous rock-hard stomach, could ascertain their whereabouts. But the sky was clouded over and when the clouds did break, and he was allowed a glimpse of the heavens he swore he did not recognize any of the constellations. At this news, the crew, a superstitious lot at the best of times took to kissing what charms and amulets they possessed and praying to their favorite gods.

Thoric being no more than a boy had no battle trophies, only the hammer pendant his father had given him for his namesake, Thor, a common enough necklace for a Viking, but he kissed it and prayed fervently along with the rest. He was a farmer's son and had little love for the sea.

Thoric didn't just pray for a fair wind and clear skies. He prayed for his very skin. Some of the Vikings had been muttering that Njord, the god of the sea, needed to be appeased. They must have angered Njord by taking Thoric aboard. It was well known the boy's father was cursed. There were murmurs of a sacrifice and malevolent looks were cast his way. Thoric was also the youngest of the raiding party and the least popular. If there was to be a sacrifice, willing or not, he knew who it would be.

It had been Thoric's first raid and a miserable one, too, nothing like the tales told around the great fire in the long hall. Thoric had loved those tales told by the bold and fearless warriors, tales of battles heroically won against overwhelming odds and ugly foes. The warriors were rewarded with caskets of gold and silver and fair maidens to keep their furs warm at night.

Thoric's father Erin had spat when Thoric had recounted the tales to him. He had said those tales didn't amount to a bucket of piss and the days of great warriors were long gone, if there had ever been any. Thoric thought it was just his father being bitter at no longer being welcome at the great hall. But after the dismal raid, he began to reconsider all of his father's words when it came to raiding.

The raid had been on an unfortified village that Balder and the other captains had raided several times before. It seemed on arrival that it might have been raided once too many times.

The only remaining villagers were either too old or too young to have fled inland. It had an abandoned desolated look. Even the cattle looked half-starved, their rib cases showing through their scraggly hides. The Vikings in the raiding party had worked themselves into such a fever pitch of blood-lust that not even a chicken had remained alive and everything on two legs had been raped more than once (including the chickens).

Children barely old enough to walk were raped, along with hags too old to walk. One Viking, Garth, always boastful of his sexual prowess, had somehow managed to penetrate a squealing babe with his member, and he paraded around the killing field with it impaled on his stiff member to peals of laughter from his fellows. Thoric would have thrown up if he had had anything left in his stomach to give. Instead, he dry-heaved while the carnage unfolded around him.

Orin, on the other hand, who continually boasted of his prowess on the battlefield, showed it to good effect by immediately decapitating a crippled old man who was on his knees, begging for mercy. As the torrent of blood showered his chest, Orin beat it with his axe and roared his war cry, which, he maintained, could be heard as far as Valhalla. He then pinned one of the old women to the wall of a hut through the shoulder with his dagger and sodomized her through her wretched rags until black shit streamed down her straddled legs. After he finished, he chopped her in half with his axe as if he were butchering a particularly scrawny and stubborn piece of meat and made another one of his famous yells to Valhalla.

The other Vikings were no better. Even Balder, whom Thoric had held in some esteem, helped himself to a young girl who could not have been more than six, before splitting her up the middle with his boat hook, starting with her now ruined and bloody cunt. It was lucky for Thoric, in a way, that the raiding party had been so intent on satisfying their cocks and blood-lust that none of them saw him creep into one of the abandoned huts to vomit his last meal—he would have been ridiculed for ever.

He knew even as he emptied his guts that the terrified cries of pain and horror from the young children as they were raped or put to a gruesome death would echo through his memories all his life. He vowed there and then to Odin and the gods of Asgard that the blood of a child would never stain his axe, but even that promise offered no consolation from the pitiful yells that surrounded him.

There was not a single treasure worth taking from the village. Even the cooking pots were rusty and filled with holes. They made do with a dozen eggs, a couple of hens, and the few head of half-starved cattle that roamed the razed fields.

Thoric wondered if even the ablest poet could find something noble to sing about this particular raid. He hung his head in shame every time he thought about it, and it was lucky that the fog had come down to hide the bitter tears that coursed down his face.

One of the raiding party, Edric, a boy barely older than Thoric and prone to acne, pointed out that Thoric had failed to rape even one woman in the unfortunate village. Thoric pointed out rather needlessly that they had been flea-ridden old hags and he would rather have fucked the villagers' scraggly livestock. There were murmurs of agreement to this from several of the warriors, who, even now, were busy scratching their groins. It might gain him a little sympathy for a while, but others were busy sharpening their axes.

It was considered ill luck to make a sacrifice aboard the actual vessel, but with no land in sight and winds blowing in several directions at once, they might have no choice. Things could not be much worse, the Vikings reasoned. But they were wrong. Things were about to get a lot, lot worse ...

It started with the steering oar. The lead oarsman could not control it. It was as if the huge oar had taken on a life of its own. The lead shouted at the other oarsman to help, but even with the aid of several of their strongest, he still could not control the thing. It threw them about like a bucking horse. One of the men was thrown with such force across the deck that Thoric clearly heard his spine snap above the winds as blood gushed from the man's mouth.

Balder swore at all of the gods' creations and ordered the crew to tie the oar with rope before it threw the ship over. It was to no avail. The oar was like a wild thing, and the ship was now spinning so fast it made Thoric's head spin. It was then that Balder let out the cry they had all been dreading: "Maelstrom! We are in the maelstrom."

The skies above grew so black, and the darkness descended so quickly that it was as if a candle had been swiftly extinguished. The steering oar snapped off the same time as the sail was ripped from the mast, and it flew into the sky like a huge bird of ill omen. Waves raging taller than the mast crashed over them. Thoric found himself waist-deep in sea water. He might not have been a friend of the water, but his father had possessed the foresight to teach him how to swim, unlike many of the Vikings, who loved and feared the sea in equal measure.

Thoric jumped over the side of the ship, which was now so flooded with water it was barely discernible from the surrounding ocean. The other Vikings, most of whom could not swim, clung to their oars and wept at their ignoble deaths.

Still, the ship spun faster and faster in the raging whirlpool that was the maelstrom, dragging Thoric down with its undertow. Then all was darkness and cold, so cold, he could not feel anything and no longer knew if he breathed air or water.

CHAPTER TWO

THE BEACH

The gull experimentally pecked at Thoric's face. Its sharp, cruel, curved beak managed to penetrate flesh and reach bone. Thoric spluttered awake with the pain. The gull squawked in surprise and flew off. Thoric sat up. His head felt like a huge boulder upon his shoulders; to move was agony. His eyes felt too heavy to open, and the thought made his head spin. And the thought of spinning made him retch. He found himself on his knees, seemingly spewing up the contents of the whole ocean. He thought he would never stop. His stomach cramped when there was no more to vomit and it finally came to an end. He opened his eyes and found himself staring at the damp patch of sand where he had emptied his guts.

He sat back. Somehow vomiting had relieved the weight of his head, but it took a while before his eyes could accept the light and for him to get his bearings. When he tried to stand, the world turned upside down. He found himself flat on his back again. He stared up at the white, cloud-filled sky and wondered if he were alive or dead.

On reflection, he decided he would not have felt the vicious peck from the seagull and definitely would not have blood streaming down his cheek if he were in Helheim, the land of the dead.

His second attempt at getting to his feet was more successful. He surveyed his surroundings. He could never have imagined a more desolate place.

The bleak, stony beach that marked the end of their small piece of farmland back home was a veritable paradise compared to the wasteland in which he found himself. The sky was milk white, the rocks black, and the sand gray. Even the seaweed marking the turn of the tides was either black or gray, depending on its age. The waves pummeling the shore were covered in the dirty scum and flotsam from a thousand shores. Every time a wave hit the beach, it retreated with a reluctant hiss. The black, boiling waters beyond signaled a vicious undertow, no doubt from the maelstrom.

Thoric moved further up the shore. He had no wish to try his luck once again in the dark waters. The beach consisted of nothing more than shingle and dirty-colored sand. Facing the sea was a high chalk cliff dotted with caves. The beach ended at both ends in boulders nearly as high as the cliff itself. He could hear the roar of the sea beyond them. The boulders formed a natural reef break. This was probably the only piece of shore for miles. It seemed he had been lucky not to have been smashed against the cliffs. He thanked Odin for his good fortune but did not forget Thor in his silent prayer, and he kissed the hammer on its leather thong.

His throat was burning from the salt water he had vomited, and he now had a deep thirst, one he knew would soon be all encompassing. Did it mean his good fortune on surviving the maelstrom and washing up on the only stretch of land was to be replaced by a long, lingering death from thirst? He had to leave the shore and find fresh water. It would mean either scaling the cliff or exploring one of the caves in the hope it led to high land.

Over the hiss of the waves, Thoric became aware of another sound quite unlike those where rock met sea. It was a loud clacking coming from everywhere at once. He banged his fist against his ears, thinking they must be full of the sea water he had not managed to swallow, until he realized it was coming from the depths of the caves and reverberating along the empty shore.

Thoric's first instinct was to explore the dark caverns and see who or what was making the noise, but a strange dread held him back. It did not take long for him to understand why his survival instinct had checked him, for emerging from the caves were things out of a child's worst nightmare. But Thoric was no child, and this was worse than any nightmare. You awoke from nightmares.

All along the deserted beach, giant crabs were pouring from the dark holes, which, he now saw, were nothing more than their monstrous burrows. Thoric looked around for somewhere to hide, but at his back was the roaring sea, on either side were the huge, slippery rocks, and before him were a horde of enormous crabs. The smallest amongst them was the size of a young pony. This, at least, settled a question in Thoric's mind about where he was. He had obviously washed up in Jotunheim—the land of the giants.

The clacking came from their huge purple and red claws, which they waved in the air in an awful harmony. Their hairy mandibles dripped a sickly green goo. Thoric had no doubt that it was in anticipation of his soft flesh. Any forlorn hope he might have clung to that he had gone unnoticed was dashed by their long eye-stalks, which were all firmly pointed at him.

He cursed his fate. One moment, the gods had smiled upon him, and the next, they had turned their backs. This was no place for a mortal, and he had a feeling that trespassers would be dealt with most ruthlessly.

As the crabs emerged from their caves, crooks, and crannies, Thoric was left with little doubt as to what their main diet consisted of—he could quite clearly make out the piles of bones and skulls, which he had mistaken for small rocks.

Instinctively he felt his belt for his axe. It was no longer there. He didn't even have his dagger. It appeared he would have to meet his death unarmed. There would be no feasting for him in the halls of Valhalla. You had to die in battle with a weapon in your hand for that. He moved slowly backward. He had no wish to appear that he was about to flee; judging by the crab's strange sideways gait and outlandishly long legs, they could move fast if they wanted to. He desperately looked around for some kind of weapon. The only thing at hand was a bleached branch that looked like it might snap at the slightest touch. But it was something. He could at least make a stand and die like a warrior.

Thoric could not take his eyes away from the leading crab's huge front claw and its razor-sharp edges. It was all too plain that they would snip him limb from limb like scissors through cloth. His bowels rumbled a warning, and he felt a thin, warm stream run down his legs, which mingled with his piss.

The lead crab was nearly upon him, and Thoric had backed away far enough, or so he thought, to give himself a clear run to the sea. He had decided he would rather drown than be torn apart by those cruel claws. But a group of faster, smaller crabs had cut him off. It looked as if the crabs were masters at this game, and they had no intention of letting their prey escape into the sea. They were carefully, purposefully surrounding him, leaving him no opening for escape.

Thoric poked at the first crab's eye-stalk but in one swift movement, the crab snipped the branch in half. Thoric threw the now useless bit of wood away and grabbed a rock, which he hurled at the crab. It bounced harmlessly off its thick carapace. He might as well have flicked a pea at it. Thoric wondered if he was fast enough to run between them and make it to the cliff. But it was as if the crabs had read his mind. They closed ranks, leaving no space whatsoever to run into. They were so close now that their dreadful stench filled the air. The crabs smelt of putrid fish and reminded Thoric of a dish favored by some southern Vikings who had once visited his village. It had made him want to puke then, and if he could have done so now, he would have been grateful for the opportunity.

He stepped back once more and balled his fists, such a futile gesture that it almost made him laugh. He waited for the leader to pounce, but for some reason, all the crabs had suddenly stopped their endless clacking and the inexorable march towards their kill. He heard it then: a piercing, shrill whistle that hurt his ears.

Thoric thought he had seen enough strange sights that morning to last a lifetime, but he was sure they would be nothing compared to what he would see as the crabs parted to let through some new horror. But it did not turn out to be the even more gigantic monster he had expected, but a wild-eyed young man with unkempt hair that reached his waist, clad in armor made from crab plates, a trailing seaweed cloak, and shoes made from conches.

The man was riding one of the behemoths as if it were a horse! If that was not strange enough, he appeared to command all the crabs by whistling, as if he were herding livestock. Thoric was just relieved that they no longer wanted him for breakfast.

The young crab-master signaled him to climb aboard the crab he was riding. Somehow, even though Thoric's legs were shaking so badly he could barely walk, he managed to haul himself up behind the young man. His savior smelled very strongly of seaweed. Thoric realized when he was up close that most of the man's clothes were made of the stuff.

The throng of crabs parted to let the riders through, forming a temporary honor guard. Mercifully for Thoric's nerves, they had stopped clacking their terrible pincers and did not look half so threatening from his lofty perch beside the crab-master. Every so often, the man would make a clacking sound at the back of his throat. He had obviously mastered the creatures' language.

The man had wild purple eyes, and it was difficult to tell where his hair ended and the seaweed began. He steered his mount, the largest of the crabs, towards the dark caverns in the cliff face. Then he and Thoric dismounted in front of one adorned with sea shells. Inside, the walls were also covered in shells, but these were multi-colored mosaics depicting a king with two sons. One of them was the young man. Thoric realized he was in the presence of royalty, but it meant little to him. From his limited experience with kings and princes, albeit of the Nordic variety, he had found them all to be self-aggrandizing scoundrels. And his father had made a point of avoiding them altogether.

A small fire in the center of the cave gave the walls a cheerful glow. The smoke rose up and outwards through a natural funnel in the cave's roof. It did not smell of the sea inside but of spring. The Crab Prince (which is how Thoric now referred to him in his head) tossed a handful of dried herbs on the fire and led Thoric to a couch made from soft moss and dried lichen. Thoric lay down gratefully. Within seconds, he was sound asleep.

He awoke to find the tattered remnants of his clothes had been exchanged for a plain white robe. He had also apparently been washed with perfumed soap, and to add to his disgust, he found that the fuzzy stubble that he had been growing for several months, in the hope it would eventually become a beard, had been shaved off.

His savior was attending a small fire while stirring a pot of appetizing stew. He smiled at Thoric and brought over a wooden bowl and spoon. Thoric feebly tried to push the prince's hand away so he could feed himself. The prince gently pushed his arm down and patiently fed him from the steaming bowl. The stew contained shrimp, delicate, small fishes, and slivers of seaweed. Thoric had never been one for seafood, but after a few spoonfuls, his stomach growled for more. He had never tasted anything so good. When the bowl was finished, the prince put a cup of sweet water to Thoric's lips, which he gulped down appreciatively. It had a faint taste of something herbal. After draining the cup, he fell back into another deep sleep.

Days and nights passed like this. Thoric felt as if he were wrapped in the soft, warm furs of his bed at home. The prince tended to him through his feverish dreams, anticipating Thoric's every need.

Finally the fever broke, and he awoke fully to find himself naked and cuddled up to the equally naked prince, who was snoring peacefully in his arms. To his immense embarrassment, he found that he was hard. The prince must have sensed his awakening, and he turned his head to give Thoric a sweet, shy smile, almost maiden-like. Then his head disappeared under the woolen blankets, and Thoric felt a delicious warmth enwrap his cock as the prince took him into his mouth. The prince's hand gently and expertly massaged Thoric's shaft and balls until he could no longer hold back the gathering rush of his spunk. His cock exploded in the prince's mouth, and he greedily and noisily sucked and swallowed every drop of Thoric's juices. A wave of happiness and gratitude swept over the Viking. The prince lay his head on Thoric's stomach, and Thoric stroked it. Then they both fell back once again into a dreamless, bottomless slumber.

The next time he awoke, Thoric found he was alone in the cave, with only the warmth and flickering shadows from the fire to keep him company.

He remembered the prince taking him into his mouth and the delicious feeling of expectation and ultimate release. To his shame, he found himself hardening, even against his will. His father had always told him that cock's had minds of their own and it was only fools that listened to them. He knew that to restore his warrior's pride, he should at least kill the young prince. But he owed the man a debt of life that would be false to repay with death. The raging battle in his head between desire and honor gave him a headache. He took a swallow from the jug of herbed water that the Crab Prince had told him eased pain. And so it did.

How many days Thoric lay eating, sleeping, and being pleasured by the young prince, he did not know. Days and nights blended into one warm, perfumed whole.

Once his strength had started to return and his wounds healed, he spent his time pacing the cave and exercising. He had made up his mind now. He would refrain from killing the Crab Prince for two reasons: he owed him his life, and if he was ever to get off the beach alive, he would need his help. There was also a third reason, one he was too ashamed to dwell on: he felt a kind of affection for the man that went beyond mere comradeship, one that should be reserved for women or shield-maidens. This now manifested itself physically. Thoric never allowed the prince to kiss or caress him. He did, however, allow him to suck his cock, but this had now progressed to fucking him in the arse.

It had started one morning as they lay sleeping. As usual, when Thoric started to wake, it was his cock that stirred first. The Crab Prince, who had his back to him, had felt the hardness and reached behind him to test its stiffness. Thoric sucked in his breath with a hiss as the prince's fingers lightly wandered up and down his cock's shaft and fingered its hole. He waited for the prince to turn and lower his head on his cock. His balls were already hardening. Every morning started this way. But instead of turning his body, the prince brought his knees up to his chest and guided Thoric's cock into his arsehole. Thoric had seen the prince naked enough times to know that his rear was a good deal firmer and prettier than any maiden's. Thoric had checked his mind several times before when it had turned to thoughts of lust, but the prince, who never spoke, had caught his furtive glances more than once, and many were the times he parted a cheek so Thoric could see the little pink hole, so like a rose bud, that Thoric knew was his for the taking.

Thoric had never expected to lose his virginity in such a manner, but such was the prince's prowess when it came to sex that Thoric had been taken to such heights of ecstasy that he wondered if he would ever desire a woman again. He also wondered what his father would make of his actions. Most Viking fathers would turn their backs in shame on a son who slept with men, but Thoric's father seldom reacted like other Vikings. Thoric could imagine his father shrugging and saying,

"What are you worried about, lad? You enjoyed it, and so did he. What's the problem?"

And that was the problem. Thoric needed to get off the beach. He needed to get back to a life he knew. He had been trying to learn the crab speech so he could tell the Crab Prince, but he had to resort to mime. It turned out not to be necessary; the Crab Prince already knew. He drew pictures in the sand to explain that the only way off the beach was on the back of a crab, as the overhang made it impossible for a human to climb the cliff unaided.

So began Thoric's lessons on riding a crab. The prince gave him a crab nearly as big as his own. At first, Thoric could not manage to mount it, but he loved a challenge. Within days, he had learned the complicated intricacies of steering the huge beast. Even though he had spent months learning the clacking language of the Crab Prince, he could still only manage the most rudimentary of clacks, but it seemed to be enough to satisfy the giant, and what satisfied the giant apparently satisfied the other crabs, as he was left the freedom of the beach to practice.

The Crab Prince would often join them to scavenge amongst the debris washed up on the shore by the maelstrom. Thoric had become nearly as expert as the prince at spearing fish caught in the roiling waves. His fellow Vikings would have mocked him, he knew, as the spear consisted of merely a sharpened stick, but he knew their mocking would have stopped when they saw how lethal he had become with it. Nothing impressed a Viking more than prowess with a weapon.

It was there, amongst a pile of rotting seaweed, while his crab was grubbing for dead fish, that he found an axe. It might have been old and rusted, but it was still serviceable. He spent several days honing it and rubbing it with fish oil until it gleamed like new.

Now their evenings, after a day of patrolling the beach, were spent poring over rudimentary maps the Crab Prince drew in the sand with a stick. Then Thoric, invariably aroused by the sight of his kneeling companion's arse, would mount the young man and spend his seed. This seemed to content his partner, who would then prepare their evening stew, which never varied much, apart from what they caught in the rock pools, but was always good.

Thoric never would have thought he would develop a taste for fish, but now he relished every mouthful. He also enjoyed the strands of the most delicate of the seaweeds, of which there appeared to be more varieties than he could count. He particularly relished a red-veined variety that made the stew spicy and hot, another thing he would never have imagined. On his father's farm, their food, apart from the occasional piece of meat, consisted mainly of bland vegetables and grains, with no hint of spice or seasoning.

Thoric's body had now become as well-honed and athletic as the Crab Prince's, and he was surprised at how easily he could move large rocks and run without tiring. Many mornings, they would run along the hard sand where the beach met the sea, their mounts clacking thunderously behind them. Finally they would lie there, exhausted, staring at the sky, until they fell into each other's arms, laughing about who knew what. It was maybe just being alive, Thoric thought.

The Crab Prince appeared in no way dismayed at Thoric's impending departure. He seemed to accept it as calmly as his arrival. It was different for Thoric. While tenderly gazing at his partner's back as the prince attended to their meal and drink, he sometimes felt a clutching at his throat that went as deep as his heart. But he dismissed such feelings nearly as soon as they came. It was not a Viking's way to have regrets.

There was only one way off the beach and it was up. The cliffs were sheer flint and slimy, and they rose into the clouds like a dark wall between heaven and Earth.

The Crab Prince had supplied him with some sort of armor, which consisted of giant turtle shells as breastplates and one as a shield. Apart from a loincloth, Thoric was naked from the waist down except for a belt, in which he had tucked his axe, and a pair of clog-like shoes made out of conch shells. He supposed he now resembled the exact strange sight that had met his eyes when he had first set his gaze on the prince.

As they stood at the bottom of the sheer cliff, the Crab Prince presented Thoric with a parting gift: a leather thong, similar to the necklace he wore from which hung Thor's hammer. It was an oyster shell, with the mother of pearl exquisitely carved into a likeness of them together. The prince took it from his neck and placed it carefully around Thoric's. After clacking some kind of goodbye and kissing Thoric on the forehead—the first time Thoric had ever allowed the prince to kiss him—he turned his crab around and left with the horde of giant crabs following him. Thoric was alone once again.

CHAPTER THREE

THE JOURNEY

From the bottom, the cliff did not seem a cliff at all. The overhang far above blocked out all light. It was sheer blackness that stretched for infinity.

For a moment, Thoric hesitated, but the crab did not. Thoric had strapped himself as firmly as possible to the saddle, and the saddle, in turn, was strapped as firmly as possible to the crab. He had prepared himself as much as possible for this moment, with hours spent standing on his head or spinning around until the dizziness had driven him to his knees. But nothing had prepared him for this: his world turned upside down, and so did his stomach. He gripped his teeth around one of the many leather reins, partly to stop from screaming, partly to suppress the vomit that was ever-present in his throat and threatened to explode with every fresh lurch the crab made. Instead of being mounted on top of a crab, it was as if he were clinging to the back of a giant spider crawling up a wall.

After a while, he did not know if he was going up, down or sideways. Closing his eyes seemed to make things worse. He concentrated instead on looking down at his saddle. The only sense he had that they might be gaining height was the wind which seemed to be increasing with every jolt the crab made.

For some bizarre reason the movements began to take the shape of the thrusts he had made into the hole of the Crab Prince, and despite his overwhelming sense of vertigo, he found himself growing hard. His father had often told him hanged men died with an erection after emptying their bladders and bowels. He had already shit and pissed himself numerous times; perhaps this was his body preparing itself for the drop, his death on the rocky beach below. The thought of death at that moment strangely comforted him. Anything was better than this constant motion, which was a thousand times worse than the sea-sickness he'd experienced on his ill-fated voyage—worse, even, than the all-encompassing swirling of the maelstrom.

The wind grew stronger. He strained every muscle to stay on the crab's back. The blast did not seem to affect the crab, which had not ceased its monotonous, repetitive clacking ever since starting the ascent, as if it were chanting to itself for reassurance.

All at once, the cyclone ceased. So did the crab's motion. Thoric felt the world righting itself as if a platter had been turned the right way up. He tore his eyes away from the saddle and looked down at grass, verdant green grass. He couldn't remember a more welcoming sight. Behind him, far, far below, he could still faintly hear the sound of crashing waves.

He carefully disentangled himself from the jumble of ropes and vines that secured him to the crab and slid off its back to kneel and kiss the ground, watering the grass with a stream of grateful tears.

Once he had regained his sense of balance, he rose on shaky legs and found that he was some distance from the cliff's edge.

The crab seemed completely unperturbed by the whole episode and was busy using its giant pincers to dig up grubs. Thoric took some dried herbs from a small pouch and munched on them. The Crab Prince had given them to him to soothe a troubled stomach and lift his spirits. Thoric gave a loud whoop of joy aimed at the cliff's edge and sat down to take in the view.

He was sitting at the edge of the world. In front of him lay the vast expanse of rolling waves, above which rushed equally giant clouds until it was difficult to tell where the sea began and the sky ended. He clutched at the grass for reassurance as if it were an anchor between that world below and his new found throne above.

His sense of well-being was short lived, however. All at once, engulfed by a giant shadow, he found himself being lifted effortlessly into the air as if by a god's hand. All of his vertigo returned as the discernible land disappeared quickly beneath him, turning into a patchwork quilt where what trees there were looked like sprouting twigs. Two enormous red talons painfully gripped his shoulders. Only the turtle-shell shoulder pads prevented them from biting into his flesh. He had no doubt he had been captured by one of the giant eagles the Crab Prince had once drawn for him in the sand. He'd expertly drawn the bird and, alongside it, the picture of a man so that Thoric could judge the relative size.

He couldn't say he hadn't been warned, Thoric thought miserably. Even so, he couldn't help thinking the picture had belied their true size and had not taken in account the thunderous squawks, which threatened to burst his eardrums. In between the eagle's shrieks and the throbbing of its giant wings, Thoric could hear the faint sound of clacking. Turning his head painfully to one side, he made out the crab, held captive by another of the monsters. He felt relieved and saddened to see his faithful mount was also captive. The eagle had cleverly caught the crab by both of its pincers, rendering it harmless. It looked helpless in the air, its legs and mandibles hanging limp as if it had accepted its fate.

Thoric realized that it was useless to struggle. If the eagle dropped him, it would lead to death just as certainly as being hacked by its cruel, hooked beak.

The eagles appeared to be heading towards some far-off mountains. It occurred to Thoric that this could only mean one thing: they were being taken to the eagles' nest, probably to feed their offspring. No doubt, some terrible fate awaited them there, or perhaps their only means of escape.

His fears were confirmed sooner than he wanted. Half-way up one of the nearest mountains, perched on a ledge, was the eagles' eyrir, the biggest nest he could ever have imagined, but what it contained was beyond his worst nightmares.

The eaglets, if they could be called such things, squawked in rapture as their parents deftly dropped their quarry into the nest. There were four of them, each one twice the size of Thoric. He backed into a corner of the woolly nest, axe in one hand, his sharpened stick in the other. By the look of it, he and the crab were not the only visitors to the eyrir. The nest's floor was littered with skulls and bones. It was difficult to tell if they had been men or animals. The bones had long ago been picked clean of any flesh they might have once held and had been bleached white by the sun.

The eaglets approached cautiously, heads darting from side to side. Thoric picked up one of the larger skulls and threw it at the nearest eaglet. It screeched in alarm and hopped back. They were evidently not used to their prey putting up much of a fight. And why should they? Their talons alone could have ripped him down the middle with one swipe, and their beaks looked razor-sharp. Just one peck, and Thoric knew he would be done for. He clacked at the crab, which was behind him, but it looked like it had gone to sleep. Thoric kicked it in frustration.

"That won't do any good," a voice said from somewhere above his head. Thoric looked up and was amazed to see a giant white bird perched on the side of the nest, busy preening its pure white feathers. It cocked its head and Thoric noticed it only had one eye; the other was a ragged hole. The bird's yellow eye gazed down on him with what looked like only temporary interest, as though Thoric were a worm and it was deciding whether it could be bothered to take the trouble to eat it or not. "You've really gotten yourself in a fix, haven't you?"

Thoric was keeping one eye on the giant bird and one on the eaglets, who appeared to be warily circling him. There was a slow, sinister purpose to their movements now. He swiftly overcame his surprise at the fact that a huge bird was making conversation with him and decided to focus on one danger at a time. He found that the bird, which had not stopped preening itself, was getting on his nerves.

"You could rescue us, you know," he said to it, "instead of just babbling on."

"Oh no, I couldn't do that. It would be interfering with the laws of nature. Besides, I don't think you've taken into account the effectiveness of your hard-shelled friend there."

Thoric glared at the bird and then glared at this hitherto faithful mount.

"He's sleeping. It's alright for him. It's me they're going to eat first."

"That just shows what bad taste young eagles have—they'll eat any old thing. Now, a well-traveled species like an albatross, a noble species of which I happen to be a member, would never pass up the chance of eating a tasty crab rather than a smelly human."

Thoric had no time to think up a reply to the insult, so he chose to ignore it. Besides, he reluctantly had to admit that the albatross was really rather resplendent with its magnificent, spotlessly white feathers. He swung his axe at one of the eaglets, which was getting dangerously close.

"I've heard of albatrosses. It's supposed to be ill luck to kill one, but I'm not one for trusting to luck."

The albatross cocked its head to the other side. "I suppose it would be ill luck for the albatross, now that you put it like that. Anyway, nice chatting with you. Things to do ... people to see ... You know how it is. By the way, you may have one of my feathers—eagles don't like them."

With that, the bird took majestically to the skies, leaving a large white feather the size of Thoric himself to flutter down next to him. Thoric picked it up, it was surprisingly light and very beautiful in its own way. He waved it experimentally at the advancing eaglets, feeling slightly ridiculous. It had an immediate effect on them. It was as if he had been brandishing a flaming torch. They backed off a few yards.

Then the hitherto supposedly dormant crab decided to make its move. With lightning-fast, deft thrusts of its deadly pincers, it neatly sliced off all the eaglets' legs, and they fell to the floor, squawking in agony.

Thoric gazed at his savior in dumb amazement. Then he stroked its shell and clacked some words of thanks. But their troubles were not over yet.

The mother eagle, alerted by its offsprings' cries, had immediately doubled back and could be seen as a black dot on the horizon, gradually and ominously growing larger.

"Now would probably be a good time to climb onto my back," said a semi-mocking voice. Thoric recognized the tone as a dark shadow engulfed the eyrir.

The albatross set them down in a dense forest far out of the sight of the irate eagles.

"No need to say thank you. Keep the feather," it said, and then it flew off without turning its head.

As the crab contented itself, as usual, with digging. Thoric tried to work out where they were by drawing in the dirt the map, which he had memorized by heart.

From what he could work out, they were somewhere in the forest that lay between the Amber Mountains and the swamp. The swamp was, evidently, full of poisonous serpents. On one side, he faced poisonous snakes, and on the other, the wrath of the eagles. Staying in the forest seemed their best bet for the moment.

They had water aplenty; on every side were streams of clear running water draining from the mountains but food was another matter. The streams did not seem to contain fish, and there were no traces of droppings from wild-life. Thoric did not like to think about grubbing for worms like the crab when their supplies ran out. He built a fire and chewed some dried seaweed to stop his stomach from grumbling, and then he lay down and slept.

CHAPTER FOUR

THE SEVEN DWARFS (but not quite)

Thoric was prodded awake by what appeared to be a very short man with a long beard, standing a long way off and with a long, sharp stick, or a very large man with a long beard and a short, sharp stick, standing very close. He rubbed the sleep from his eyes. It turned out to be, for all intents and purposes, a dwarf with a long stick who looked extremely annoyed with him for some reason.

Thoric reached instinctively for his axe. It was not there.

"Is this whit ye'r keekin fur, laddie?" the dwarf said. He tossed the axe casually in the air and nonchalantly caught it without looking in a clearly practiced manner.

"Is this whit ye ca' an axe? Ah wouldn't uise it tae cut mah butter. Whit urr ye—human? Nae muckle o' a specimen. A'm inclined tae murdurr ye if it wur nae fur that muckle beastie yonder. Is it yers, or urr ye tis neist bridie?"

The dwarf produced a nasty-looking dagger so that Thoric could follow the general gist of things.

"Now, now, Grumps, is that a way to greet a traveler in our forest?"

Another dwarf had appeared alongside the one who was still prodding Thoric experimentally with the stick. But this one looked almost respectable compared to the wild-eyed dwarf by Thoric's side.

The only strange thing about the friendlier of the two dwarfs was what he wore on his nose: some kind of polished glass discs held together by wire. Curiosity got the better of self-preservation. Even though there were only two dwarfs, they were well set and armored. All Thoric had was a secreted razor-sharp clam shell, which was only useful in close quarters, a sharpened stick, and a feather.

The crab seemed to be taking no interest in the events, as usual, but nevertheless, Thoric moved slightly closer to it. He had no real experience with dwarfs. What he knew was only from stories and legends. They were supposed to be incredibly swift and cunning. He decided to satisfy his curiosity about the strange things upon the dwarf's nose and hopefully relieve the tension, which was mainly emanating from the one he now identified as Grumps.

"What are those things on your nose?"

"They are called spectacles. They help me see." The dwarf removed them and handed them to Thoric, accompanied by much grumbling from the other dwarf, who looked at him suspiciously, as though he were going to eat the things. Thoric tentatively placed them on the ridge of his nose, as he had seen them on the dwarf. He blinked; everything had turned into a blur. He hastily removed them and gave secret thanks to the gods that his eyesight had returned to normal. He gave them back to the older-looking dwarf who replaced them on his nose.

"What you just glimpsed is how I see things without them."

Thoric nodded, although he was not sure he understood. Clearly, though, this was a dwarf of much wisdom and craftsmanship.

There was something that had been bothering Thoric since his encounter with the albatross, and that he was now experiencing again with the dwarfs. He instinctively felt he could trust the dwarf with the spectacles.

"How is it that you speak my language and even birds can talk? Am I mad? Am I dead?"

"Ye should be," growled the other dwarf, stroking Thoric's axe rather lovingly now as though he wanted to test it on Thoric's neck.

"I think you should come with us," the friendlier dwarf said. "I think I can answer some of your questions but not all."

Grumps spat in disgust and threw Thoric's axe into the undergrowth.

Thoric was getting used to wonders, but now dwarfs on top of it all! He must be dead, surely. But how to find the halls of Valhalla in this strange dreamland where everything seemed more real as every day passed?

The dwelling the dwarfs led him to was as pleasant a place as he could ever have imagined: a small cottage that looked like it had been constructed and reconstructed many times. He felt like a giant as he stooped to enter.

Inside were five other dwarfs sitting around a low, sturdy oak table.

"Let me introduce ourselves. I'm called Doc. You've already met Grumpy, and these are Dopey, Sneezy, Bashful, Sleepy, and Happy"

They all gave the impression of living up to their given names. Dopey was trying to scoop soup into his mouth using an upturned spoon, Sneezy was appropriately sneezing every few moments and wiping his nose on an already-soaked sleeve, Bashful wouldn't look at Thoric, Sleepy was asleep, and Happy just grinned at him.

"So what do you do here," Thoric said, "farm?"

The question was greeted with general mirth. Even the dwarf called Sleepy woke up for a moment and managed a sleepy smile.

"Our food comes from an allotment where vegetables grow all by themselves," replied Doc. "It was planted by our Snow White, who is bewitched and cannot wake."

"Could I see her?" Thoric asked.

"Of course. You aren't a prince by any chance?"

Thoric confessed he wasn't.

"Whit a surprise!" Grumpy said.

Doc took him back outside and walked him to a clearing in the forest. In the middle was a glass casket containing the most beautiful woman Thoric had ever seen. She was surrounded by piles of precious gems of all descriptions. Her hands were crossed over her chest, and she did, indeed, appear to be in a deep sleep, although, only the occasional rise in her chest proved she was breathing at all and not completely dead.

"Why does she stay like this? Why can't she wake-up?" Thoric asked.

"Because it is our story, and in our story, she can only be awakened by a kiss from her Prince Charming."

"'N' that ain't ye laddie," came the rumbling tones of Grumpy who never seemed to be far behind Doc. The other dwarfs were slowly filing into the clearing as well.

"Why do you say it is 'your story'?"

"Before I answer that, tell me how you came to be here?" replied Doc.

"I was on a ship, and we were caught in a whirlpool. I ended up on a beach. It was full giant crabs, and just when I thought I was going to be eaten, I was rescued by a man who knew how to control them. He gave me a crab of my own." He nodded towards the giant, who was, as usual, grubbing the earth in search of worms. "Although I'm not sure *it* knows it. *It* does its own thing most of the time."

Thoric left out his close relationship with the Crab Prince and the amount of time they had spent in the cave together. He was not so overly embarrassed about having lain with a man now, especially one who had offered himself so readily. It was the fact that he still hadn't been with a woman. And then there was Grumpy. Thoric had never been good at lying. He knew instinctively that any crumb he let slip would be seized upon by the cantankerous old dwarf. Thoric could just imagine the scornful taunting that would follow such a revelation.

He quickly proceeded to tell of his adventure with the eagles and the talking albatross and, how he and the crab had been dumped unceremoniously in the forest, where the two dwarfs had found them.

"That's jobby," said Grumpy. "No one haes ever git aff that beach alive. Whit kind o' lying pumpin' wizard urr ye?"

"He speaks the truth. How else would he have the crab?" Doc said, taking off his spectacles and wiping them with a cloth. "He has no reason to lie. If I'm not mistaken, you are a Viking, aren't you?"

"How do you know that?" Thoric asked.

"Doc kens everything," Grumpy said as he spat in the general direction of the crab.

"Take no notice of Grumps here. I don't know everything. If I did, we wouldn't be here."

"And where is 'here'? Thoric asked. "Am I near Valhalla, because I'm surely dead."

"You are no more dead or alive than we are. As to the proper name of this land, I have as much an idea as you do. We know it as Film, but it does not sit right, as that was the name of the place we came from. For the true answer, you must seek out the Pale Lady. They say she knows more about this land than any other. She lives in a castle beyond the mountains."

"'N' she's guarded by a dragon," growled Grumpy. "Sae, guid luck wi' that. Mibbie we'll find yer bones, 'n' ah kin carve me a crakin' axe."

Thoric stared at the mist-covered mountains in the distance.

"I have seen the place on a map."

"You have a map?" Doc looked surprised.

"Not really a map. More of a picture drawn in sand."

Grumpy gave out a bellow of laughter, and Happy followed suit. Soon most of the dwarfs were rolling around on the grass, laughing. They finally stopped, stood up, and re-arranged their clothing.

"Th' laddie haes a map made o' sand," Grumpy said. "He mist needs keep it in a poke sae it doesn't git drookit."

This comment started the dwarfs off again. Only Doc and Thoric weren't laughing. Thoric because he didn't understand a word that Grumpy uttered and Doc because he never laughed, only smiled. He was smiling now.

"What did he say?" Thoric asked him.

"That you need to keep your sand map in a bag so it doesn't get wet."

Thoric nodded slowly and stared down at the dwarfs as they rolled on the ground with mirth. Vikings weren't big on humor.

"Those must be the Amber Mountains." Thoric pointed to the eponymous mountain range outlined in orange across the horizon. "The castle of the Pale Lady lies the other side, does it not? It will be difficult to cross them. I think it's where the eagles live, and they've a score to settle with me."

"Who said anything about going over the mountains? We are dwarfs and we mine. We go under the mountains. There are tunnels. First you need to eat and sleep."

Thoric's stomach audibly growled at the thought of food.

"Weel, he ain't sleeping 'n' eating at our place. He belongs oot 'ere wi' that monster o' his," Grumpy said.

"Of course he will stay with us. There's always much to learn from travelers. Take no notice of Grumps here. He has a heart of gold, really, and a more loyal friend you would never find."

Grumpy turned his back on them and farted loudly to illustrate his view on the subject, and then he stalked back to the cottage.

"Take no notice of Grumps. He's ..." Doc said, beginning his now-familiar litany.

"... Got a heart of gold, really," Thoric finished for him.

They both laughed, and Thoric patted Doc affectionately on the back. He found he was taking a great liking to the wise old dwarf. He clacked at the crab, and then he and Doc rode back to the cottage on its back. The crab didn't seem to mind.

Grumpy trailed, spitting and muttering to himself, in their wake. Thoric noticed that where there had previously been no sign of woodland creatures, they all seemed to magically appear wherever Doc made an appearance. The jolly dwarf appeared as popular with animals as he was with humans.

For the next few days, Thoric was left alone to recuperate. He spent most of the time resting and joined the others at meal-times. The food was good and plentiful, and so was the ale, which the dwarfs brewed themselves—mostly Sleepy and Happy—which explained a bit how they'd gotten their nicknames.

Thoric kept himself fit by going out every day to chop wood or help in the extensive kitchen garden. Thoric had worked on his father's farm enough to know how to grow things. He marveled at how good the soil was; everything thrived as a result. There was an orchard of various fruit trees. Some he recognized, but most were unknown to him. His main job was to "aerate the soil," as Doc put it. As with a lot of things Doc said, Thoric had no idea what he was talking about.

The aerating consisted of a pair of well-made boots with large nails set in the soles, which Thoric wore to march up and down between the trees. According to Doc, it helped the earth to breathe. Thoric wondered about this for some time as he trudged up and down between the trees. Finally he asked Doc if he meant the earth was alive.

Doc kneeled in the grass and signaled Thoric to do the same.

"Touch the ground. Do you feel anything?"

Thoric did as he was told. He shook his head.

"Underneath your hands are hundreds of thousands of small animals, each one going about its business. A thousand farmers could not do the work they do. And amongst them, the worm is king. You never know how many there are until you till the soil or it rains. Do you know how to summon worms, Thoric?"

Thoric shook his head once again.

"Hmm, it may come in handy one day. Watch." Doc placed his hands on the ground a foot apart. "Worms react to vibration. That's why they emerge when it rains. The raindrops warn them the earth could become flooded and they'll drown. So, to summon the worms, you must use your fingers like raindrops."

Doc started tapping an odd rhythm with his fingers. Sure enough, worms started wriggling to the surface. At first, it was just a few of the fat, sluggish creatures blindly searching for the missing raindrops, but then dozens started to pop up.

Doc moved to another piece of grass and squatted down with Thoric.

"Now you try," he said.

Thoric put his fingers to the ground and tried to copy what he could of Doc's rhythmic tapping. Nothing happened.

Doc put his hands over Thoric's and moved his fingers for him. In no time at all, the ground was smothered with worms.

"Practice," Doc said. "You'll soon get the hang of it."

So, every day, Thoric practiced the little-known art of worm summoning. Soon he was as adept as the wise old dwarf. Thoric did not question why Doc thought it would prove to be useful to him one day. He had learned not to question Doc. Whenever the sage dwarf said something, it inevitably proved to be correct.

Sometimes, Thoric would make a game of it, seeing how many he could get to rise to the surface. If he summoned too many, he would clack to the crab, who would make short work of the worms, which it seemed to relish nearly as much as the fat grubs it dug for.

The one thing the dwarfs loved above all else was stories. After supper was the time for stories, which were usually told by Doc, but now they had Thoric and his adventures. But even more than his experiences, they loved hearing about the gods of Asgard and the dwarfs of Nidavellir. These particular dwarfs were also known as black elves and they were master blacksmiths.

Grumpy pretended not to be listening by keeping his back turned the whole time, but Thoric noticed he always kept himself within earshot. Thoric told them the Viking tales his mother had told him as a child, especially the ones about Thor, his namesake.

Thoric soon became restless again. The dwarf's home was even less "real" than the Crab Prince's cave, and he knew instinctively that the longer he stayed, the harder it would be to depart.

Doc's recollection of the dwarfs life before they had met Snow White only served to confuse him more. The dwarf told of an extremely colorful two-dimensional world full of music and songs, which they all knew the words to, although they had never learned them. They had all known they were part of the "story." They'd no free will. Then Doc would launch into one of his weird speeches, peppered with words Thoric did not understand, like "robots," "pre-ordainment" and "scripts."

Then, Doc told him, there had been a fire, one so intense that the world had melted around them. Then they had awoken here, somehow still in the "story" but not. This place was more real than the other place had ever been, yet none of them aged or died, and by Doc's calculations, they had been here centuries.

The idea that time had no meaning in this world resonated with Thoric. When he had left their village, he had still had the baby fluff of a beard. But even now, nothing had changed. When he looked at his reflection in still waters, he looked exactly the same, yet he knew much time had passed.

His father had told him that if he really wanted a beard like a true Viking, he should shave the "bum fluff" off and finally he would get a strong growth, but then it would become a pain in the arse as he would have to keep it constantly trimmed if he wanted to appeal to any of the young maidens. Everything was "a pain in the arse" to his father. They had never been exactly close, even less so after Thoric's mother had died, but every time he thought of his father, it would bring a pang to his heart. He longed for his father's gruff company more than anything else. If anyone knew what to do in his situation, it would be his father.

He missed his home. The key to getting there, apparently, lay with this "Pale Lady." He would find her and ask her the way.

CHAPTER FIVE

THE DRAGON

It was time for Thoric and the dwarfs to say their goodbyes. The trek through the tunnels under the Lonely Mountain had been a long one, just Doc, Grumpy, and him. Tunnels went off in every direction, lit by gems placed at strategic points and exuding a twinkling, multi-colored, subterranean light. Doc led the way as if he had trod it a hundred times. He probably had. Thoric thought to himself.

There was finally sunlight at the end of the tunnel.

"You will be safe from the eagles now," Doc said.

"Bit nae fae the dragon," Grumpy said. "Ye micht need this."

He handed Thoric a package. It contained the most beautiful axe he had ever seen. The handle was covered in carved runes, but its blade was so bright it could not be looked upon long.

"Thank you, Grumpy. I don't know what to say ..."

"Then clam up, you eejit. Ye aye did say awfy much."

With that, Grumpy squeezed past the crab and disappeared down the tunnel.

"May your gods go with you, Thoric, son of Erin," Doc said, and followed Grumpy down the tunnel.

"What about the dragon, Doc?" Thoric called after him.

"Don't worry about the dragon, Thoric. It will find you. Go safely."

It took some time for Thoric's eyes to grow accustomed to the bright sunlight after the artificial light of the tunnels. He blinked his eyes several times and the scene gradually took focus. What stretched before him was a wasteland full of boulders and sand. The empty sky was relentlessly blue in all directions, as though a stranger to any cloud.

The only directions Doc had told him were to bear right when coming out of the tunnel and always make sure that rocks lay ahead of him.

The advice seemed nonsensical now. There were rocks in every direction in fact, rocks were the only thing that broke the monotonous horizon.

He mounted the crab. As ever, it seemed to know which way to go without prompting. It turned automatically to the right, following a trail only it could see. Every so often, it would stop as if to take its bearing. Its eyes, on their long stalks, would sway back and forth as if searching for something; then, with a satisfied clack, it would resume its awkward sideways progress.

Thoric looked up into the sky, hoping the sun would give him some sort of bearing or even a stab at the time of day. But there appeared to be no sun, just the blinding blue sky, which, if he looked at it too long, made him feel dizzy. The place seemed as empty of sound as it was of shadow.

He had heard of places called deserts from wandering Vikings, but they had spoken of hills of sand like waves in an ocean. They had told him that just like the sea, the desert had its own moods, its wind and storms. But here the very air was so still that not even a grain of sand moved except for the ones they shifted in their passing, and even those settled back into their place. After a few moments, there was not a trace of their passing.

The place should be hot, Thoric felt, but it was neither warm nor cold, as if even temperature did not belong in this place. The boulders were the only things of any interest in the whole horizon. But they only varied in shape and size; they all had the same uniform gray color. Some were truly enormous, larger than many houses stacked one on another, and others were no bigger than Thoric's toes. After a while, it seemed to Thoric he had seen the same boulders many times before. They must be going around in circles. It was only logical given that the crab only moved sideways.

He tried clacking to the crab and steering it to a different course, but the crab did not respond, and in the end, he let it have its way. He supposed that if he were to die here, it was as good a place as any. It was a reflection of how he felt inside— a vast nothingness, devoid of hope.

They would not die for a good while yet, though. The dwarfs had provisioned them well, even going so far as to provide two large sacks of dried grubs for the crab.

Thoric was not sure how long they had been traveling, but the rumbles in his stomach told him to eat. He clacked the crab to stop, and this time, the crab obeyed. He dismounted and scattered a large handful of the dried grubs on the ground, and then he sat and ate dried fruit while he watched the crab delicately pick at the grubs with its small mouth mandibles, which were no bigger than Thoric's fists. Thoric drank some water and wondered, not for the first time, how the crab survived without drinking. Maybe it drew moisture from the air, but there was surely no moisture here. He gave up the question and fell into a doze, lying against the crabs back.

The vibrations had stopped. The dragon slightly shifted its huge ungainly body. No, not stopped completely. He could feel the man-meat's heart beating even from this distance. The other thing had stopped its movements at the same time. It brought with it a faint tang of the ocean, a smell the great worm loathed. But the man-meat's smell was another matter. It made its mouth water. It flicked its tongue once more out of its burrow to savor the air and sank back down, deep down, to await their movements. Then it would commence its burrow towards them. The man-meat would make a tasty morsel. It had been so long since the dwarfs had sent it a treat.

After their rest, the crab and Thoric ambled on into the blue oblivion. Now, at last, the land showed signs of change: large pits in the sand, which the crab carefully circumnavigated. Bleached skulls and bones surrounded the pits, but from a distance, even Thoric, with his keen eyesight, could not make out if they were human or animal. He felt a strange reluctance to use the eyeglass to confirm his suspicions.

The boulders near the pits told their own story. They were scorched black. Thoric knew enough about fire, as did all his kin, to know that the heat that had blasted the rocks must have been many times greater than even a smith's furnace. So, here was the first sign of the dragon. The breath of fire was something he had heard of in the legends of his people. But the stories that were told were often confused, and truth to be told, he did not think any Viking alive had really seen one.

Thoric had a horrible feeling he would probably only see the dragon for a few seconds before he was burned to a crisp.

"That weren't richt, Doc, 'n' ye kens it," Grumpy said as they navigated their way through the tunnels.

"Don't say you have developed feelings at long last, Grumps?" Doc replied, passing him a dried apple.

"Ah ainlie kens whit's richt 'n' whit isnae."

"You've never complained about so-called princes and dragon-slayers before."

"He weren't na dragon-slayer."

"And he wasn't a prince, either, as you so aptly pointed out. But I have a feeling about this young man. He might just be the one. And as you very well know, in the end, if he had opened the glass coffin and tried the kiss—we would have ended up burying him along with the rest. This way, he has a chance to reach his Valhalla, as he calls it, and die the hero's death he wanted."

"Heroes!" Grumpy spat in disgust. "Ain't hee haw heroic aboot bein' brunt tae a cinder."

"That's as it may be, but we are still in the 'story,' remember? We all have our parts to play. Anyway, you did give him your best axe."

"Dinnae remind me. That's whit comes o' gettin' tae lik' someone. Ah loved that axe."

"Well, I'm sure either the dragon or Thoric will appreciate it."

"Wilnae git it me back, though, wull it?"

Doc smiled benevolently at Grumpy's back as the dwarf continued his relentless mutterings through the tunnels.

One day, they would really have to do something about the dragon, he thought.

If there was a dragon it seemed to be making itself pretty scarce, Thoric thought as he and the crab circumvented their way around the pits.

Thoric decided it was time to put his and Doc's plan into action before they were taken by surprise. It was time to make the dragon come to him.

He chose the largest of the boulders, where the scorch mark had only succeeded in marking its base. The crab needed no prompting. It climbed it as easily as it had climbed the cliff. Thoric never ceased to wonder about his crab. It seemed to know Thoric's thoughts better than he knew them himself.

Thoric dismounted at the top and took the bags from the crab's saddle. Then he took the stick from his back, which he had, with the help of Grumpy, fashioned into a double-headed spear. Its twin steel heads were horribly barbed and razor-sharp. Making weapons seemed the only thing that gave Grumpy any pleasure, though, of course, he would never admit it.

The spearhead was made of silver. According to Doc, dragons disliked silver intensely. If they craved any metal, it was only gold. The spearhead glinted in the bright light, and for the first time, Thoric noticed the cunningly wrought runes engraved on it, as if they had come to light of their own accord.

Grumpy was indeed a master craftsman, and Thoric wondered, as he had many times, if he were not somehow related to the family of Brokkr and Eitri, the dwarfs who had fashioned Mjolnir—the mighty hammer of Thor. But Grumpy professed no knowledge of Svartalfheim, the realm of the dwarfs, which lay beneath Midgard. He only spoke of some legendary god named Disney, who had been the creator of their former world. But Thoric always noticed a strange light come into Grumpy's eyes when he was at his forge and Thoric spoke of the legendary brothers.

He set the bags beside him. One contained pebbles, and the other a deer's heart, beloved by dragons more than any other meat, Doc had said. The meat, once he unwrapped it, was very ripe and stank. Even the crab moved away a little.

Thoric then smeared the paste that Doc had made for him over himself and the crab. Supposedly, it would disguise their smell from the dragon. How, Doc had not explained. It smelled of nothing, but that was probably appropriate for this still, silent place, Thoric thought. Lastly, he put on his grass-treading boots. Careful not to stand so as not to blunt the nails, he crawled towards the edge of the boulder and swung his legs over.

Then he started throwing the pebbles around the pit in a steady rhythm, much like Doc had taught him to summon worms. Last of all, he threw down the deer's heart.

The great worm was burrowing in a frenzy now. It could feel the vibrations around one of its burrows, which meant that the prey was caught in its shifting sands and would not be able to escape. But there was also something even more delicious than the man-meat falling into its pit. The man-meat was carrying the most delicious of treats, and it must reach him before the greedy creature ate it himself.

At last! The sand in the pit was shifting of its own accord. The dragon was coming. Perhaps this was the moment Thoric had always been waiting for. This was the chance to become a real warrior, to die fighting and to redeem himself as a Viking.

However, Thoric was not prepared for the horror that emerged. He had expected a fierce, scaly, snake-like creature with wings as depicted in Viking carvings of dragons, not the eyeless, sickly yellow head with its gumless mouth and the terrible stench that accompanied it.

It slid smoothly out of the hole and made unerringly for the deer's heart. Its tongue flicked out and expertly tossed it into its mouth. The hairless head, with its eyeless sockets, swung backward and forwards. It was seeking him, Thoric knew. He threw more pebbles at the base of the boulder. The head shifted toward the sound, then came what Thoric had been waiting for. The two black holes that passed for its nose spurted a long jet of flame at the base of the boulder.

Thoric, perched at the top of the boulder, felt the blast of heat and its sulfurous stink. The worm-like dragon heaved more of its sickly, bloated body from the hole. No doubt, it was expecting to find the charred bodies of its prey. The tongue flicked here and there, searching. The dragon seemed confused, shaking its head to and fro, its tongue flicking out more and more now.

Thoric chose his moment carefully. His months of practice with the spear would pay off now or never.

The dwarfs, for once, were sitting around their evening meal in silence. The only noise was the crackle of the fire in the heath and Sleepy's snores.

For once, it was Grumpy who chose to speak first.

"Ah wonder howfur th' boy's daein'? "

Thoric was on all their minds. Even Happy, forever optimistic, looked forlorn.

Doc looked up from his untouched stew.

"It's what he chose. See, dying does not matter too much for Thoric. That much, I have gleaned from his culture. It's the manner of his death that is important to him. It must be a hero's death to enter his treasured hall of Valhalla. What better way to die than in battle with a dragon. He carries a private shame that he would not reveal even to me. If he lives, he will remove that burden from his mind forever."

"Howfur wull we ken. He's nae aff tae fin' his pumpin' wey back 'ere, is he?"

"Snow White will let me know," Doc said.

The dwarfs all knew that Doc had some secret link with the sleeping princess.

This seemed to satisfy Grumpy who noisily started in on his stew. The others slowly followed suit. Happy grinned.

"I think he will beat the dragon!"

"He'll be th' foremaist pumpin' yin if he does," Grumpy said, stating the obvious.

Thoric was in the same mindset. He threw the spear with all the force he could muster. He knew that if he failed, it would mean his death. It hit exactly where he wanted—right through the dragon's tongue. The dragon let out a great bellow. Doc and Grumpy had been right. The dragon didn't like it at all.

The great worm found it could no longer shut its mouth and create the gases it needed to breathe fire, nor could it retreat underground with its mouth wide open—the sand, once its friend, would suffocate it. The lidless, sightless eyes turned red with fury. The spear had pierced straight through the middle of its forked tongue and was now firmly lodged there, embedded in the bottom of the dragons mouth, and when he had tried to close it, the spear had equally buried its sharpened end in the top. It's cruelly crafted barbs lodged deeper the more the dragon struggled, causing it more agony.

The dragon beat its head against the base of the boulder, trying to dislodge the spear and also seek its prey. It was then that Thoric jumped.

He landed squarely on the back of its neck, feet first, his boots digging deep into the fat, blubbery skin. Then he set to work with his axe, striking over and over again into the soft muscle at the back of the great worm's head. Putrid yellow flesh finally gave way to crimson blood welling up through the hole he was digging.

The dragon had stopped moving altogether. It seemed to be in a state of shock as if something was slowly dawning on it. It summoned all its strength and started wriggling its loathsome body backward towards the pit. It must have decided that the best way to remove the irritating thing clamped to its back was by taking it underground, even if it meant running the risk of suffocating itself in its own barrow.

Thoric realized at the same moment that he would no doubt die along with the dragon in its hellish hole. But he had not counted on the crab. While Thoric had been busy plowing a furrow through the dragon's neck, the crab had scuttled down the side of the boulder and was underneath the belly of the worm, where its body was at its softest, slicing through it like butter with its huge claws. As the dragon moved slowly backward, it was leaving a trail of its own steaming, stinking entrails, full of excrement and half-digested meals.

The dragon started to shudder violently. Its head was moving backward and forwards, but slower now, as if in bafflement. It tried to roar, but it could only manage a gurgle. Thoric was now knee deep in blood and gore, hacking through bone. He recognized that pinkish-gray brain matter that was now beginning to emerge from the cracks in the dragon's skull.

It knew something was terribly wrong. The pain that had made it so desperate was slowly receding. It could not move its body any longer, and its brain was stuck in a mire. It felt itself receding as if it were being swallowed whole by the dark earth at last.

Finally the great worm stopped its spasms. It dissolved until it was nothing but a puddle, and there, at the center, stood Thoric and the crab. For the first time, Thoric truly embraced his fearsome friend.

CHAPTER SIX

THE ASGARDIANS

Loki could hear Thor's roars of laughter before he even got to the gates of the Great Hall of Valhalla. He wiped the frown from his forehead and prepared to meet the jibes of the other gods, especially his red-bearded brother, with equanimity.

"Ah!" roared Thor as soon as he spied his brother. "The man of the moment. A tankard for my brother. I think he needs to drown his sorrows."

Loki accepted the tankard of frothing ale as graciously as he could manage under the circumstances. He downed it to the mocking laughter of the other gods.

"Thoric outwitted you, Loki. That takes some doing. Shame on you, a mortal outwitting a god! He managed to make your so-called dragon worm food."

This was greeted with warm chuckles. The gods knew to obediently laugh if Thor was in a good mood. It was known as playing it safe in Asgard.

"There will be another," Loki said. "You don't know much about the great worms, Thor."

"I know a dead one when I see it!" Thor roared again amidst another peal of laughter from his appreciative audience.

"Cut off its tail, and it will grow a new head," Loki said.

"All the more fun for Thoric to kill it again. And now he will have his prize: a real woman at last. The Pale Lady, a woman befitting a Viking warrior."

"C'est la femme," Loki sneered.

"And what does that mean?" Thor grew suddenly serious and tightened his grip around his ever-present hammer. "Not another one of your evil incantations. You know you are not allowed to use spells in this hall."

"It's nothing, just a human phrase. It means: *There is always the woman.*"

"Yes, and her cunt will be a damn sight better than anything he's had before. Not jealous, my brother? Surely, he fucked you enough times up the arse in that cave of yours to satisfy even you. It's a wonder you didn't get crabs!"

Another bellow of laughter, and many gods followed suit, thumping their tankards on the great table in appreciation (although they kept a weather eye on Loki, who was known to harbor a grudge, for centuries sometimes). It wasn't often that Thor managed some semblance of wit, and Loki was not sure if he hated that more than he hated the death of his "dragon" or that Thoric was still alive.

"We will see. Even cunts get boring sometimes, Thor." With that, and with a swirl of his black cloak, Loki left the hall.

Thor didn't know how deeply his words had cut Loki. He had loved Thoric, and the pain of his departure from their little love nest had only been replaced by the need for vengeance to placate his hurt feelings. Loki, a god, who had given Thoric more pleasure than any human could ever have expected, had been thrust aside like some old hag. The eagles, meant to be his swift and powerful vengeance, had been thwarted by an albatross. It had not gone unnoticed by Loki that the albatross had been blind in one eye, just like their father Odin, but even Loki would dare not infer that their father would lower himself to interfere in such a trivial matter.

Loki paused on his walk home to think more deeply. Why would Odin take an interest? It had only really ever been a competition between Thor and himself as to who would gain the mortal's affection. And in the end, in his witless way, his brother had triumphed, but only with Odin's help. And their father only ever helped a person for one end—his own advantage.

CHAPTER SEVEN

THE PALE LADY

The landscape began to change. Very subtly at first. So subtly that Thoric barely noticed. Something in the air. Slightly more humid. No more giant, monolithic boulders. No more pits and no signs of scorching.

When he saw the first signs of grass Thoric dismounted and picked a blade. The taste flooded his senses. He was a young boy again, running through the meadows of his youth and then lying down, panting, to stare at the sky and chew on the first grass stems of spring—it was the taste of life and freedom. Even the crab seemed happy, clacking enthusiastically as they moved forward.

Grass gradually turned to saplings, and saplings to trees. There were plants but still no sign of animals. There was moisture in the air, and clouds had started to appear but they were static, suspended in the air as if by invisible threads. Thoric longed for rain. He had been rationing his water carefully, but now he only had one flagon left. He knew that if they did not find water soon, he would die of thirst long before hunger. He knew that where verdant things grew, there must be water, but it must be far underground. The crab seemed to know where they were going, and Thoric had long since ceased to try to steer it. He did not bother to dismount to sleep any longer. He slept in the saddle, never knowing night from day.

While dozing in the saddle, he saw a forest and a distant mountain. He knew he was dreaming because it was twilight and there was no twilight in this place. He could hear the babbling of a stream, so he definitely knew it was a dream, but it was a pleasant one, so he let it go on. It was only until his senses told him that they were no longer moving that he reluctantly opened his eyes, only to find they were already open—it was no dream.

The crab was clacking impatiently. Thoric wondered how long he had been in his daydream state. But it no longer mattered, for in front of him was a clear stream. He had never thought that the sight of running water could bring him so much joy. Since his birth he had always been surrounded by water in one way or another, and like so many things, he realized it was the very things you took for granted that were missed most keenly.

He jumped to the ground and threw himself into the water. It was ice cold, but he did not care. He was a Viking, and Vikings did not know the meaning of cold. He drank deeply. The water was so cold it bit his throat. He clacked for the crab to join him, but there was no need. The crab was already immersed in the stream as much as its giant body would allow, clacking softly and contentedly.

Night was beginning to fall as they emerged from the water. Just as the water had seemed a miracle that he had so longed for, he hadn't realized how much he had longed for darkness. He shook himself like a dog and did some swift exercises to warm himself. He fed the crab and ate the small amount of the food that was left for him. He wondered if he might soon be joining the crab in eating grubs. He dressed and lay down next to his faithful mount, which, for a supposedly cold-blooded creature, was extremely warm. He gazed up at the unknown stars. His father had once told him that on one of his journeys, he had met an alchemist from the East who had told him that the stars were so far away that it would take many lifetimes to reach even the nearest one, even if you flew as fast as the swiftest hawk. As he fell into real sleep, he wondered vaguely if his father was seeing one of those stars and wondering what had become of his son. He hoped he wasn't feeling sad.

The next morning, as the sun came up, despite his precarious situation, Thoric was glad to see it and eager to go deeper into the forest, towards the mountain. If there was a castle, it was sure to be on top of the mountain—everyone knew that. He filled the flagons with water, and they set off.

The raven tapped impatiently on the Lady's bedroom window. It rarely slept, and the habit of human beings to lie horizontally unconscious for seven or eight hours a day not only frustrated the bird but annoyed it, especially when it was bearing tidings—important tidings at that.

The somnambulant figure under the white, silk sheets gradually began to stir. The woman yawned, stretched, and slowly climbed out of bed. She gave the raven a rueful look and opened the window. It hopped in with an equally reproachful croak and went straight to its perch and ate some corn kernels.

The woman seemed undecided about whether to return to bed or sit at her dressing table. Finally she settled on the latter and proceeded to brush her long blonde hair. She looked at her reflection in the mirror with her pale, gray eyes. It was just habit, she knew, as the reflection that greeted her had not changed for countless centuries. The same pale face with its mournful look and slightly slanted eyes stared back at her. She yawned again and drummed her fingers impatiently on the table while the raven ate its corn. She knew it was deliberately keeping her waiting because she must have kept it waiting while she slept. She let it have its petty vengeance. She knew of old that ravens bearing news could not wait to let loose, to discharge it, as much as a man with constipation longs to shit. But her raven was old. It had learned to withhold its information until it was good and ready. She could, of course, with a wave of her hand, make it talk whether it wanted to or not, and the raven was wise enough not to keep the Pale Lady waiting too long. Some of her spells could be extremely painful, and that was when she was in a good mood. If she was vexed, well, that was a different matter entirely, as Snow White had found to her cost.

The raven hopped onto the woman's shoulder and croaked into her ear. It had been so long since she had smiled that she had often wondered if she had forgotten how to. She found it was not so difficult as she had imagined.

The forest was much denser than Thoric had thought when he'd seen it from a distance. It was so dense, in fact, that many times, he lost sight of the mountain altogether, and if he had not had his axe with him and the help of the crab's large pincers to cut their way through, he was sure he would never have penetrated it more than a few yards.

They came across a small glade, and at last, Thoric saw his salvation—rabbit burrows. He climbed off the crab and looked at the droppings—he would make traps. But there was no need. The rabbits came hopping out of their burrows to greet him.

That night with his stomach full of freshly roasted meat, he lay gazing contentedly into the fire. He wondered about the rabbits and their lack of fear. It could only mean there were no other predators in the forest, or none that ate rabbit, anyway. He decided to rest there for a few days to gather his strength and stock up with provisions before moving on.

In one of the nearby trees, the dark eyes of a raven twinkled in the dark.

CHAPTER EIGHT

LOKI'S REVENGE

It wasn't until the first rays of dawn lit Asgard that Thor left the Great Hall of Valhalla. He was staggering slightly. The ales had been good and strong enough to leave even him feeling the worst for wear, but it was nothing a good fuck with Sif wouldn't cure. He felt himself hardening even now under his britches.

He whistled some half-forgotten tune. What a good night. Loki's face! And it would be a better day. He looked forward to telling Sif all about it. After the fuck, of course. He pondered which of the many ways he could take her, and by the time he reached the house, he had decided on one: he would ride her from behind, pulling on her long blonde braids until she screamed with pain and pleasure—she liked it that way, but more importantly, so did Thor.

He went straight to the bedroom, meaning to catch her before she awoke.

The bedroom was empty of Sifs.

"Shit," he thought. Oh well, she would be cooking breakfast, and his stomach was growling. He would have her after breakfast, or maybe at the same time. He grinned to himself and then went to the kitchen, but there was still no sign of Sif. He started to get angry. It was by far the easiest of his emotions to have and the one he was most accustomed to. Gone were the thoughts of sex and food, replaced by rage.

He went into the garden. On a bench at the far end of the carefully kept garden was a bald woman with her back towards him, wearing a mourning shroud.

"Woman!" he bellowed, loud enough for any living thing within miles to run for cover. "Where is my wife?"

He approached the woman, whose shoulders were shaking with sobs. If there was one thing Thor hated even more than ice giants, it was grieving women, and he had left many widows to grieve. He hated it as well because it took the edge off his temper.

"Woman," he said in what he thought was a soothing voice, "have you seen my wife, Sif?"

The woman turned. Her face was streaming with tears. Thor rocked back on his heels, which was unusual for him, even when he was in his cups. Behind the tears, the bald woman bore his wife's face. She fell into his arms, and Thor knew then it was really his wife. Women only usually fell into his arms when they fainted with fear.

He felt the top of her bald head. It was completely hairless and smooth as an egg.

"But your hair, Sif?"

"It's all gone. I woke up this morning, and I felt something was wrong. When I looked in the mirror—this."

Sif's hair had been the envy of all the female gods in Asgard, as fine and blonde as new-mown hay, and its smell had been as equally delicious.

"But where has it gone?" Thor felt ridiculous as soon as he asked the question.

"I don't fucking know! Do you think it decided to take off for a stroll around Asgard? I looked on my pillow, and there is not even one hair. It has just disappeared—as if by magic."

At the word "magic," Thor suddenly regained all his slow wits.

"Loki. It was Loki."

"You can't know that, Thor. Why would your brother do such a thing?"

"Don't ask. I know my brother better than you."

Thor's voice was quiet now, and Sif knew, as did many others to their cost, that this was when he was at his most dangerous. His words were as cold as if they had been spoken by an ice giant. Despite being in his warm embrace, she trembled.

He let go of her and returned to the house. He pulled out his belt, Megingjord, which doubled his already prodigious strength. Even without it, he could defeat any god in Asgard. He put up his arm and his ever willing hammer flew into his hand. This time, he was not going to merely punish Loki—he was going to kill him.

Loki could hear Thor bellowing his name as far as his secret hiding place. Thor was charging about like a maniac on his goat-driven chariot, (which was not unusual for his brother). What was unusual was the undertone to his voice, an icy menace that made even Loki fearful. He had gone too far. He knew it.

He had acted on impulse, which was out of character for him. It had felt good at the time, cutting off every single lock of Sif's hair and shaving her head clean. It had even felt good watching the locks of shiny hair burn. But it was only a petty vengeance to hurt Thor, and now he felt deeply sorry for Sif. She was a good-hearted, loving woman. He should know; he had bedded her more than once in the guise of Thor, and many a time, it had been on his mind to utter some witticism or even something romantic into her ear. Something his imbecilic brother was quite incapable of and something the intelligent Sif deserved. But that would have given the game away.

Now he was left with the consequences and though it was very difficult to kill an immortal, Thor's hammer could hurt. Loki had been on the receiving end of it more than once, but it had never been wielded with the rage he could hear in his brother's voice. Loki lowered his head. Sometimes he despised himself.

There was only one thing for it, he would have to leave Asgard for a while and return when his brother had cooled down, however long that might take.

Thor drew up his chariot outside Loki's house. He knew his brother would not be at home. The cowardly bastard would have sneaked off somewhere. It was his wife, Sigyn, Thor wanted to talk to. He stomped to the door and smashed it open. Sigyn came rushing down the hallway, and though it stretched for many miles, she was there in seconds.

"Thor! What is the meaning of this? You have woken every god in Asgard with your ravings. Are we at war?"

"Where was Loki last night?"

"He was with you in the hall. You should know that. From what I heard you spent all night there."

"He was there but a short while. When did he come home?"

Sigyn furrowed her brow. There was one thing about her: she was incapable of lying, unlike her husband, whose lies and truths both tripped easily from his tongue.

"You know Loki, he comes home when the mood takes him. I'm sure you will find him or him you. You are kin; he would do anything for you. If he comes home, I'll tell him you're looking for him. But I'm sure he knows by now, as does most of Asgard. I could hear you shouting for him from here."

Thor looked into the Sigyn's innocent eyes.

"Yes, he'd do anything for me or against me," he growled.

He stomped back out of the house and in a moment of misgiving, he turned his head and said, "Sorry about the door."

Sigyn nodded and vanished down the vast hallway.

Loki cautiously approached Heimdall. It was always best to approach the guardian of the gates to Asgard with some sort of self-preservation in mind. There was no way in or out of Asgard without his approval, except, perhaps, for Odin.

Loki was about to give a discreet cough to the massive back of the god, who appeared to be staring out over the rainbow bridge, when Heimdall, without turning, said,

"What do you want, Loki?"

"I need to make a visit. You know, distant relatives and all that. Wish I didn't have to leave, but one of them is doing poorly. And you know the ice giants, they get offended quickly, so for the good of Asgard I must make haste."

Heimdall turned to face him.

"Thor is looking for you. See him first. Unless, of course, you want to go by me."

There was just a touch of eagerness in Heimdall's usual monotone voice, which Loki did not like. He also didn't like the way Heimdall was caressing the hilt of his legendary sword, Hofund. Although Loki was a skilled swordsman he knew he was no match for Heimdall. One of Loki's many skills was accepting defeat with equanimity. He knew when to back down. Better to face Thor even in his wrath.

"Oh, is he? My brother must need my help. I will attend to it immediately and return."

Heimdall turned his back on him again, and Loki ground his teeth. How he would love to stab the bastard in the back, but Heimdall was all-seeing. He would have Loki's gizzards on the end of his sword before Loki took a step. One day, Heimdall, we'll see about those eyes of yours, one day ...

Thor wasn't difficult to find. Loki only had to follow his thunderous roars of "Loki!" and graphic descriptions of what he was going to do to him when he found him.

Thor pulled up in his goat-driven chariot. Loki was standing calmly in the middle of the road with his arms folded. Thor got down, tapping his deadly hammer against his palm.

"I couldn't help but hear you were looking for me, brother," Loki said.

"I am going to break every bone in your body, Loki," Thor said. "And then I am going to do it over and over again until you are pulp," he added nastily.

"Brother, what is it? What have I done to offend you?" The innocence in Loki's voice temporarily disconcerted Thor, and for a moment his rage was replaced by doubt.

"Sif's hair. What did you do to it? You foul creature, how dare you call me brother!

"Sif's hair?" Loki looked bemused. "What about Sif's hair?"

"It's all gone. She's completely bald. Only you would be capable of such evil."

Thor started to pound his hammer on his palm again. What were just trifling blows for Thor would have knocked a man's head clean off.

Loki continued to look so confused that Thor's doubt returned. Then he saw something on Loki's shoulder that swept all doubt from his mind. He plucked it from Loki's cloak. It was all the evidence he needed. He hung it in front of Loki's face. It was a strand of Sif's hair.

"And what is this?"

"It's a strand of hair, Thor. It must have blown onto me from you. You did arrive in rather a dash."

"It's one of Sif's hairs."

"Is it?" Loki asked, holding it up to the sunlight as if to study it, although he would recognize the color anywhere.

"You are sure this is Sif's?"

Thor was turning a very alarming crimson.

"Yes, I'm fucking sure! Right. It's hammer time!" Thor started spinning his hammer to build up its speed.

Loki took a step back. The hammer was making a sinister whirring noise that was all too familiar to Loki.

"Wait! Stop Thor! For Sif's sake!" Loki screamed at the top of his voice.

The whirring slowed somewhat.

"What about Sif?"

"If this is really one of Sif's hairs, then I think I know a way to restore it."

Loki was thankful that the whirring slowly came to a halt.

"How?" Thor asked.

"I need to visit the dwarfs."

CHAPTER NINE

THE CASTLE

The raven knew where the Pale Lady was as soon as it saw the library window open. It flew straight onto her shoulder and cackled in her ear. She nodded. The raven went to the dish of corn that had been put out for it at the far end of the long reading table. It cocked its head to one side as it ate, studying its mistress as she pondered the huge map that covered half the table.

Her movements, to those who did not know her, appeared leisurely, almost disinterested to the point of lethargy, but she moved as slowly and purposefully as a cat, not wasting a single motion of her lithe body. She wandered back and forth between the myriad of bookshelves, picking books at random, skimming a few pages, and then returning them to their place. Then she would go back to the table, make some notes in her neat, precise hand with quill and ink, and return to studying the map.

The forest was starting to thin at last, much to Thoric's relief—and to the crab's, who made satisfied clacking noises. Thoric was well prepared for the mountain. One thing he had learned from his father was to be prepared. Norse farmers led a precarious life. Food was never guaranteed. They had to contend with the harsh and changeable weather to grow anything or keep healthy livestock. And if that was not bad enough, there were always the raids from outlaws or other Viking tribes. It was why his father kept secret stores in many different locations, not all of them near the farm. Most of the outlaws or Vikings who attempted to raid the farm learned to their cost that Thoric's father was still a skilled and cunning warrior. Very few survived, and those who did reported back to their counterparts that it was a place best to avoid.

Thoric had smoked and dried rabbit meat, and he also had venison after coming across a deer as equally pacified as the rabbits.

There was a clear path that led up the mountain to the castle. Thoric had never seen a castle in real life. He had only heard about them from his father and other veteran Viking warriors. But they had spoken of formidable stone fortresses with sheer walls only broken by slits to loose arrows. They were difficult to attack. The best way, if an army had the equipment and the patience, was to lay siege to them. Although Vikings could make many things, they severely lacked patience—except, perhaps, Thoric's father, who was the most patient man Thoric had ever known.

The Pale Lady's castle did not resemble any of the descriptions that Thoric had heard from any Viking except his father. Thoric's father had been on the raid on Paris in his younger days, and he had told his son of the wondrous buildings that the Parisians had erected to worship their god. Cathedrals, they called them. And from the way his father had described these magnificent palaces that contained their god, with narrow turrets, pointed arches, flying buttresses, and beautifully colored glass windows, there could not have been a more apt name for the residence of the Pale Lady.

The castle looked simultaneously both ancient and new, a bit like everything else in this strange land, Thoric thought. The path up the mountain was as bare and barren as the land of the dragon. It would take several days to climb. Thoric was glad to have the dried meat and refilled flagons of water.

The steep march up the wide path was as uneventful as the surrounding scenery was monotonous. The only change was the growing magnificence of the Pale Lady's castle. It now dominated the skyline. Built of pure white marble, when the sun caught, it dazzled the eye. Thoric calculated it must have at least a hundred rooms, but there was never a face at any of the many windows. The only sign of life was a large raven flying back and forth. Thoric wondered if it was relaying messages. It was said they were able to do that. Either way, he decided it must be good luck. Odin himself had two ravens, Huginn and Munnin.

He wondered, not for the first time, if the Pale Lady was incredibly ugly or suffered some deformity that made her remain so isolated. Could it be that she had been trapped in the castle because of the dragon for so long that she had withered and died?

Thoric only knew that if she was alive, he had to fuck her, ugly or not. It was his right after defeating the dragon: all the legends said that was the way it happened. He didn't intend to ask permission, anyway. He did not want to die having only known sex with a man, and he did not want to enter Valhalla as some sort of fuðflogi. He would never be able to look his father in the eye, for his father, of all the Viking warriors he knew, would surely have a seat there.

There had been a fuðflogi in Berufell, Thoric's village. He was called Alva, a girl's name, as he had been mistaken for a girl when he had been born because his male parts were so small as to go unnoticed by the half-blind, ancient midwife of Berufell.

Alva would flounce around the place, wearing women's garb and flirting with the menfolk. Thoric knew that a lot of the young village lads took him before finding a woman they could call their own. Many found him more attractive than Eira, the obliging, grossly fat widow who would take any man for a coin or even an egg. Thoric had found himself slightly attracted to Alva, who was far too pretty to ever be taken for a man.

He had been so ashamed of his lustful thoughts for the fuðflogi that he had gone, shame-faced to his father to ask his advice. His father, as always, had surprised him by remaining completely unperturbed.

"It's only natural at your age. Hell, I used to get a hard-on looking at a sheep's arse when I was your age. You should go to Eira. She'll be only too glad to accommodate a strapping young lad like you. She's well practiced in taking virgins—she might even let you have it for free."

"But she's disgusting. At least Alva is comely."

"Yes, and Alva takes more cocks up his arse in a day than Eira does in a week. And Eira's clean. She looks after that cunt of hers; after all, it's her livelihood. I've known men whose cocks have rotted away and who've gone insane after being with a promiscuous fuðflogi. There's nothing wrong with a fat woman. When you shut your eyes, all cunts feel the same. We used to say, "Any port in a storm," when we was out raiding."

Thoric had mused on that saying until he thought he understood what his father meant, but by the time he had worked up the courage to go to Eira, all his thoughts had turned to his first raid.

The great door to the castle was wide open as if he were expected. Thoric had his axe ready in case it was an ambush. The crab shared his concern and sidled in cautiously.

Thoric could not help but gasp when he took in the full size of the entrance hall. It was so huge—and he was used to huge by now—that the ceiling disappeared into mist. There was no furniture that he could see, and there were also no doors. Just one enormous snow-white marble staircase

Thoric would not have been surprised if the steps had been carved for giants, such was the scale of everything around him, but they were human size. It spiraled upwards into the mist. Thoric dismounted, and the crab followed close behind as they mounted the stairs. He counted 150 steps before they came to the first landing. It was dominated by one of the many colored windows that he'd seen from the outside. Inside, the light streamed in, turning the air into a rainbow of colors. The window depicted an idyllic scene. A naked man and woman sat in a delightful garden beneath a tree, sharing an apple. They were both ebony-skinned and flawless in their physical perfection. Thoric thought it the most pleasing thing he had ever seen.

Once he had torn his eyes away from the window, he saw that the landing had archways on either side. He chose the left one. They passed through several identically empty rooms, each with a window depicting scenes from the idyllic garden. There were no doors, only the arches separating them. Passing under one of the arches, Thoric noticed that above and around them were inscribed nearly invisible runes, which he did not recognize. His soft leather boots made no sound on the marble floor, and even the crab scuttled with only the daintiest of clicks. The place seemed as deserted and empty as an ancient tomb after grave robbers had made off with its contents, including the corpse.

It was after passing through the ninth such archway that Thoric saw that the room opened onto a balcony. He suddenly realized how much he longed for the taste of fresh air and the touch of a soft breeze on his cheeks. The silence and stillness of the castle were unnerving.

The balcony, immense as the rest of the castle, had a view so spectacular that Thoric almost fell to his knees.

It was the garden, the same perfect garden depicted in the windows. Thoric immediately longed to be there. There was only one thing for it. They would have to retrace their steps, exit the castle, and go around it, and he would be there. Climbing down would be impossible, even for the crab. The walls were as sheer and smooth as ice itself.

"You can't do that," said a soft voice behind him.

He swung round, only to be taken further aback by the sight of a tall, fair-haired woman with eyes the color of gray shadow, clad in a simple long white gown. Even the crab was startled, and it clacked nervously but made no attempt to attack the woman.

"Welcome, to my castle, Thoric, son of Erin. I am the Pale Lady."

CHAPTER TEN

LOKI AND THE DWARFS

The raven alighted on a branch in the wood that surrounded the seven dwarfs' cottage just as the sun was rising. It blinked and hopped to the ground. Out of the wood stepped a man in a long, hooded black cloak and carrying a staff. He strode purposefully to the door of the cottage and rapped on it with his staff.

It was Happy who opened the door but his usual smile disappeared when he saw the cloaked figure and the color drained from his face.

"What the fuck ...?"

"What the fuck to you, too, moron. Wake up, Doc. I have work for you." The man stepped through the door, uninvited, and sat at the head of the table.

The seven dwarfs and the cloaked man stood around the glass coffin staring down at Snow White. The dwarfs were nervous. They were always nervous when *he* came.

"I understand that her hair still grows," the man said.

"And her nails," Doc said.

"Did I mention nails?"

"Na, bit if tis juist th' locks that ye be interested in, ye shuid say whilk kind. We cuts 'n' shaves her a' ower ilka moon caw," said Grumpy.

The man swirled around to face Grumpy. From under the darkness of the hood two red pinpoints of light, burning like fire, glared at him.

"Did I ask you to speak? Even if it is fucking gibberish!" The dwarfs felt a cold wave of dread flow over them. Each of them shuddered, some inwards and some outwards. Grumpy, unusual for him, bowed his head and stared at the ground. Only Doc remained unmoved.

The man or demon—the dwarfs, were never quite sure which; they, only knew he could change shapes at will and was responsible for them being where they were—turned to Doc.

"Brokk," he said, addressing Doc. Another of the man's many foibles was to call them strange names that, though alien, seemed somehow familiar. And now they seemed even more familiar after having heard Thoric's tales of the dwarfs of Svartalfheim. But Brokk did rhyme with Doc, so the dwarf took no offence, and even he would not have dared risk the man's wrath by questioning it. Doc had seen him turn men to stone just for giving him a funny look.

"I presume you keep *all* the hair? From her *head*." He glared once again at Grumpy.

"Every strand," Doc replied.

"Good, because it is strands I want to talk to you about. Show me the hair."

Doc led him to one of the many bulging extensions that had been added to the cottage. It was full of a multitude of sacks. Doc pulled one down from a shelf and opened it. The man buried his hand in the silky black locks.

"This will do," he said.

"For what?" Doc asked.

The man produced a strand of hair from under his cloak and handed it to Doc. The hair was as fine and silky as Snow White's, although the complete opposite in color. Whereas Snow White's hair was as black as night this strand of hair was as bright and golden as freshly cut hay.

"I want you to fashion me a wig the same length and color of the hair you hold."

Doc pondered the strand of hair.

"The length is not a problem, but to get this color will require much experimentation."

"I also want it to grow into the scalp so it remains permanent."

"That will be even more problematic," Doc said.

"It is well within your capabilities, Brokk. A trifling task, in fact. How long will it take?"

"Come back in one week. I should have something for you by then."

"You will not have something. You will have ready what I asked for, and it will not be in a week. It will be completed in three days when I return."

Before Doc could make any sort of protest. The man held up his hand.

"Or would you prefer to writhe in agony for eternity in the flames I rescued you and your comrades from?"

With that, the man turned on his heels and disappeared into the wood. As soon as he was surrounded by the gloom, he changed back into a raven and flew off in the direction of the Pale Lady's castle.

The Pale Lady lay with her head in Thoric's lap. Thoric lay with his back against a weeping willow. A perfect lake in the perfect garden stretched out before them. A pair of perfectly white swans drifted slowly and silently past, barely making a ripple. Thoric had been dozing, and he guessed, from her steady breathing, so was the woman. He adjusted his position slightly. His right leg was going to sleep. The smell of their sex floated up to him on the cool air. They had spent what seemed like many hours fucking, over and over again, with only some very surprised-looking animals for company.

"Do you want to get up, Thoric?" she said.

He caught a glimpse of the cherry-red tongue darting from between her immaculate teeth. He felt his breath catch as he remembered the unbelievable pleasure he had recently enjoyed when those same lips had been wrapped around the shaft of his cock. Her tongue had seemed to be everywhere at once. Whatever sexual experience he had gained with the Crab Prince was forgotten, washed away by the great tides of pleasure the Pale Lady's body poured over him. She was a great teacher, and there was never a more willing student than Thoric.

"No, I was just making myself more comfortable," Thoric lied. He wanted to add "my love" but he was scared the Pale Lady would see him as a fool and the boy he really was.

With a start, he suddenly realized that throughout their days of hectic love-making, he had never asked for her name.

"Can I ask you something?" he said.

"Anything you want."

"What's your name?"

The Pale Lady's brow furrowed as she considered the question. She took so long in answering that Thoric wondered if she had forgotten the question and was dozing once more.

"I had a name once but it was so long ago I've forgotten. In those days, my skin was as dark as coal."

She propped herself up on one arm and looked him in the eyes with a slight smile on her lips.

"What name would you like to call me, Thoric, son of Erin?"

He had already given the matter some thought, and he already knew the answer; it was the name that had sprung to his mind as soon as he had set eyes on the Pale Lady.

"Asgerd," he said with certainty. It was his favorite woman's name. It had been his mother's name.

"Asgerd," the Pale Lady said, rolling the name around her mouth as if she were tasting a new wine. "Asgerd, it is then, only you may call me that. To everyone else, I am the Pale Lady or Lady."

When the Pale Lady said, "everyone else," Thoric could only presume she meant the servants, who consisted of a few maids and a cook. He was certain there were others. Often, he caught shadows moving mysteriously in the background, going about their mysterious duties.

The cook, a tall, thin woman with a lazy eye, prepared different and delightful meals every day. They consisted solely of vegetables and fruit. The Pale Lady forbade anyone from killing any animals in the garden. The only exception to the rule was the crab, who was allowed to roam free, digging up worms and grubs to its heart's content and catching the occasional fish. Thoric spent his time fucking to his heart's content.

The Pale Lady's lust seemed never-ending, and so was her patience. Thoric, since the very first time he had bedded her, had a problem. He would climax within seconds—he couldn't help himself. Sometimes it happened so quickly he spent his seed before entering her. Within a few days, the Pale Lady had taught him how to withhold the moment of climax and, more importantly, how to use his tongue between her thighs.

The days flowed by in a torrent of passion. They only stopped fucking to eat, sleep, and walk in the garden. To the Pale Lady, it brought back memories of times long since passed. To Thoric, it seemed as if he had truly reached Asgard, and if it wasn't Asgard, then it was as close to paradise as he was likely to get.

The raven alighted on the window sill and squinted through the steamed glass. They were at it again! Didn't they ever stop? They were worse than rabbits. As the raven flew off in disgust, its eyes glittered with hatred and fury. Its only consolation was the fact that Thoric had been taking her from behind, and not just like an animal—he was fucking her arsehole. The raven wondered if it brought back some good memories for Thoric. After all, arseholes were just arseholes, whether they belonged to a lady or a prince.

CHAPTER ELEVEN

SIF'S HAIR

Loki waited until Thor left his home before he approached the front door.

Sif answered it. The servants had been dismissed for the tine being to prevent any gossip. She was wearing a knotted scarf around her head.

"Why Loki! It's such a pleasure to see you," she said.

People who did not know her might have thought she was being sarcastic, but that was because they had no idea of her true character.

Sif was as incapable of telling a lie as water was of running back up a waterfall.

Once again, what little conscience Loki had and the little store he kept of it gave him an annoying prick.

"Sif, I have something for you," he said.

"Oh, good," Sif said, clapping her hands like a little girl. "I love surprises. I've been so down lately. You can't imagine, Loki."

Loki coughed in embarrassment but then pulled himself together and took out the wig from under his cloak. Sif caught her breath in amazement. It was truly a work of great art. The dwarfs had excelled themselves. The beautiful hair glittered in the sunlight.

THE PALE LADY · 85

"It's wonderful," she said, feeling the texture. "It even feels like living hair."

"That's because it is, Sif. It's enchanted hair. Once you put this hair on your head, it will grow into your scalp, and you will never have to worry about it again."

Loki pulled out a chair. "Come. Sit, and I will arrange it for you."

Sif sat obediently at the kitchen table while Loki massaged some paste into her scalp. He then carefully placed the wig on her head.

The sensation was strange. Sif felt as if a thousand tiny mosquitoes were all burrowing into her head at the same moment. She squirmed and felt like tearing the thing from her head.

"Sif, you must keep still," Loki commanded. "Allow the magic to happen."

Sif obediently stopped squirming, much to Loki's relief as it had visibly aroused him. It reminded him too much of how she squirmed in bed, trying to find different parts of her cunt for his cock to enjoy, which he, in the guise of Thor, skillfully penetrated to her gasps of satisfaction.

Finally the irritation stopped. Sif sighed in relief. So did Loki. He produced a hand mirror and gave it to her.

"Look."

Sif whooped in unconcealed delight. Not a hair was out of place, and the color shone with a vibrancy that even surpassed her previous hair. She ran her fingers through its silky smoothness.

"It's wonderful, Loki," she said. "And you say it won't fall off?"

"You won't even lose a hair. I promise you. Pull it and see."

Sif gave her new head of hair a tentative tug. Loki was right. She could feel how deeply anchored it was in her scalp.

"It's incredible!"

"You will never need to cut or even brush it. It will remain perfect in every way."

"How can I ever thank you, Loki?"

Loki could think of several ways, all involving his cock, but he kept them to himself.

"You are my brother's wife and, as such, my sister. Your happiness is reward enough."

She stood up and embraced him and planted a kiss on his forehead.

"You are so kind and wise, Loki. Only you could have found a way to do this."

Loki shrugged his shoulders and smiled modestly

"It was nothing. And it's no less than the most beautiful woman in Asgard deserves."

"Wait until Thor sees it!" Sif said excitedly, ruining the mood for Loki.

"Sees what?" A deep, recognizable voice said from behind Loki.

Loki stood aside so Thor could see his wife. Thor stood still and gaped, his mouth opening and closing like a fish out of water.

"I told you, brother," Loki said. "You should have more trust in me."

"I trust you about as far as I can throw you. And if you don't want to find out how far that is, I suggest you leave now."

"Such ingratitude. But I'm used to it by now," Loki said, nevertheless making a hasty exit.

Sif was about to speak, but Thor placed a finger on her lips.

"Shush, wife. We have unfinished business in the bedroom." With that, Thor picked up the giggling Sif in his arms and carried her to their bed.

CHAPTER TWELVE

EXCALIBUR

Thoric and the crab sparred with each other in the garden. The Pale Lady watched with some amusement from her balcony. Thoric was using a staff in one hand and the axe in the other. He had tied cloth around the lethal edge of his axe so as not to harm the crab. But it would probably have made no difference because, try as hard as he might, Thoric was hardly ever able to land a telling blow with either the axe or the staff.

The crab, despite its monstrous size, moved with uncanny speed and could have nipped off any one of Thoric's tender body parts at will. It showed its intelligence by just clacking at Thoric when the young Viking left any part of his body exposed and feigning what would have been a lethal cut. It seemed to enjoy the game and was an ever-willing opponent.

As for Thoric, in the early days, he had attacked the crab recklessly, and when he had become frustrated, he had expended all his energy in needless ploys to get behind the crab, who would then trip him up and tower over him, clacking in triumph or mirth (it was hard to tell with the crab).

Now Thoric was a much more cunning opponent. He did not expend the slightest amount of energy in any movement, and when he did move, it was lightning-swift and decisive.

The Pale Lady wondered at this peculiar race of men who called themselves Vikings. They were raiders and plunderers at heart and seemed to enjoy nothing more than a good battle, but at the same time, there was something remarkable and honorable in them. Thoric seemed to embody this paradox. He would spend just as much time taking out his aggressive lust for battle in mock fights with the crab as he would learning how to unravel the mysteries of the Pale Lady's huge library.

She was gradually teaching him to read and write, not just in his native Nordic but in many other languages. He was especially fascinated by the sciences and mathematics. At first, he would have nothing to do with them, believing them to be some kind of dark magic, but he gradually overcame his distaste, and the more he learned the more avid a student he became. He told her that he found science much stranger and interesting than the myths and legends he had heard. Sometimes the only way to separate him from the books was to lure him to her bed so he could satisfy her. She was not terribly keen on having a bookworm for a lover.

She had allowed him to grow a little older so that he might have the beard he had longed for, and of which he was now overwhelmingly proud. She halted its growth and his aging at the right moment. She wanted an experienced and worldly man as her lover, but she did not want him old or decrepit. Mortal men aged very quickly, and she had not tired of him yet.

She watched him walking back somewhat dejectedly from his mock battle with the crab, who had once again beaten him soundly. The crab had wandered off, no doubt to fill its belly with worms, snails, and the odd fish.

It was time to see if Thoric was really worthy of the next step.

Thoric decided he would bathe his sweat-covered body and then go to the Pale Lady's bed to restore his spirits, and then, perhaps, he would down a mug of ale before they ate. He was surprised to find the Pale Lady standing before him. She never visited the garden when he and the crab were sparring. She smiled at him, took him by the hand, and led him to the lake.

"I think you need a sword, Thoric. I know, at heart, you treasure your axe and a hammer like your namesake, but there is another way of fighting."

Thoric was always eager to hear anything about new ways of fighting.

"I have tried the sword, but it is not much good in close combat, Asgerd. The axe is better," he said.

"Not with this sword. I doubt any enemy will pass beyond its reach. But this sword has to choose you, and many have waited at the shores of this lake and been disappointed."

"What happened to them?"

"I ended up throwing their bones into the lake."

"Then I won't wait very long."

"It doesn't really work that way, but you will see for yourself."

They stood by the shore of the lake. After a while, Thoric, as usual, became impatient, but every time he went to open his mouth the Pale Lady put her finger on his lips to silence him.

A ripple started for no apparent reason in the center of the lake, spreading outwards as if something were rising. And it was. The tip of a sword was rising from the waters. It slowly rose and approached the shore. What magic was afoot, Thoric did not know, but try as he might, he could not take his eyes away from the vision, and it was not just his eyes that were stuck to the spot; it was his whole body. Try as he might to free himself from this motionless state, he could only stare at the full magnificence of the sword as it grew closer and closer until the hilt was revealed. Grasping the hilt was a hand strewn with weeds from the lake's bottom. It was unmistakably the hand of a woman, even if it was covered in weeds and mud.

The hand drew back and threw the long-sword with incredible strength into the sky. Thoric watched as it spun in the air and then plummeted downwards, heading point first for his skull. There was no way he could avoid it. He watched his doom approaching as time slowed down until all he could see was the tip of the sword, which became smaller as it approached until it was just a dot, so perfectly balanced was this sword of death.

It landed squarely at his feet and half-buried itself in the ground instead of his head which it would, no doubt, have penetrated just as easily.

"It likes you," the Pale Lady said.

"How do you know that?"

"It did not kill you. Now it's yours. Take it."

They returned to the castle, with Thoric carrying the sword. It was extremely light when he carried it, but when he tried a few exploratory swings, it became incredibly heavy. The sword was bereft of any markings that he could see. He suspected no mortal could inscribe anything on the unknown metal—that is, if it had been made by mortal hands.

"Its name is Excalibur. You can read about it if you want, but first you need to learn to use a two-handed back sword. I have just the person," the Pale Lady said, reading his thoughts, not for the first time.

"He is called a Samurai," she explained stopping before a strangely dressed individual wearing a fearful-looking mask.

"Is he alive, then?" Thoric asked. "I always thought it was a statue."

The warrior-cum statue had been transported out of the library and was now in one of the many empty rooms.

"Being completely inanimate is a state that only very few men can master," she said.

"So, he's not dead, then?"

"Thoric, when will you realize that in Ultima Thule, being dead or alive is merely a perspective."

Thoric hated it when the Pale Lady spoke of such things, which she termed metaphysics. It always ended up giving him a headache. He preferred things cut and dried: dead or alive, night and day, black or white. These in-between states, which seemed quite common in Ultima Thule, clouded the whole issue. Thoric preferred not to dwell on them.

"For now, he is under implicit instructions not to kill you, but he may hurt you. Each session will become progressively harder until you become a master." With that, she left the room, leaving Thoric to ponder on the words "for now."

The samurai were Japanese warriors—he had read about them in the Pale Lady's library. He had not been able to read about them in their own language; he had enough difficulty with the European alphabet without trying to tackle the strange runes that made up Japanese writing.

Thoric much admired their strict code of honor, their indifference to pain, and their unflinching loyalty. These were all great merits to a Viking. The samurai's shogun, he presumed, must be the Pale Lady, although it was highly unusual for a samurai to swear fealty to a woman.

The samurai had his long-sword strapped to his back in much the same way as Thoric. He tapped the samurai's armor to see if he might wake up The samurai didn't move.

Thoric stepped back and drew his sword, holding it in two hands, though it was incredibly light for its size. As far as he knew, though, it was the best way to hold a broad sword. It felt strange to be without a shield.

The samurai came to life with the drawing of the sword, and it bowed to him. Thoric immediately saw the lowering head as an opportunity to lop off the samurai's head. The samurai jumped back as the sword swished through the air where his head had been.

"That was extremely disrespectful. Next time, you will bow to your master," the samurai said.

"I have no master."

"A rōnin," the samurai spat in disgust. "I should have known. That's why you have no honor."

With that, the samurai slightly shifted one foot, and before Thoric could react, the samurai had disarmed him and put his slightly curved sword to his throat.

Then, with the flat of his blade, he proceeded to beat Thoric to the ground.

"Now, rise and bow, rōnin, and recover your weapon."

So began Thoric's first lesson in the ways of the samurai.

CHAPTER THIRTEEN

THE BUILDER

Thor, now content that Sif was happy once more, had decided to renew his on-going argument with the trolls. He had left Asgard, heading east and looking for a fight.

This was quite normal for Thor, who would often find Asgard too peaceful for his restless and bellicose nature. The other gods were quite relieved in a way. It had been brewing for some time. Thor, instead of his usual jovial self, would sullenly sit in the Great Hall and stare into space as if willing some god to be foolish enough to pick a fight with him.

Asgard was a duller place without Thor, and many of the Aesir were sage enough to realize it was also a far less safe place without the flame-haired god of thunder. Thor was the bulwark of their defense against their many enemies. They might have the rainbow bridge, Bifrost, the only entry into Asgard, and the mighty Heimdall guarding it, but even he could be overcome by sheer numbers. Thor, though, was always the first into battle and could always be relied upon to rally all of the gods to follow him (mainly because they didn't want to get beaten up by him if they didn't).

Odin sensed the unease and decided it was time to act.

"We need to build a wall," he said. "High and thick enough to repel any invader, be they troll or frost giant."

"Then it would need to be an enormous wall. It would take us years to build and think of all the work," Loki said. (Loki hated manual labor of any kind.) "And the cost!" (He was also extremely mean.)

"Nevertheless, we still need a wall," Odin said He rose, which put an end to any discussion. They would be building a wall.

The very next day, a stranger arrived in Asgard seeking an audience with Odin. He was plainly dressed and had something of the brawny smith about him. His cart horse was a poor specimen. It looked about to drop dead. The outline of its ribs showed through its scrawny hide.

Odin looked at the pair distastefully."What can I do for you?"

"I hear you need a wall," the stranger said. "I can build it for you."

Odin looked at him scornfully. "I don't know how you heard about that, but it's beside the point. How many workers do you have? And if I was actually reckless enough to give you the job, how much would it cost and how long will it take?"

Loki was aghast. "You can't be taking this clown seriously?"

"Shut it, Loki. Let the man speak," Odin said.

"Workers! I don't need them. I just need my horse. I'll have it built by the first moon of next winter."

The gods bayed with laughter.

Odin held up his hand to silence them. "And the cost?"

"I want merely three things: the sun, the moon, and the hand of Freyja in marriage."

Heimdall drew his sword. "I will kill him for his impertinence, All-Father."

"Hold, Heimdall," Odin said. "Wait outside for a moment while we discuss this matter," he told the stranger.

The stranger bowed respectively and left the Great Hall. As soon as the door had closed behind him, all the gods began shouting, sometimes to Odin and sometimes at each other.

Odin held up his hand and the hall grew quiet again. He turned to Freyja. "What say you Freyja?"

Freyja was considered the wisest and one of the most beautiful of the goddesses, and her words always carried weight

"I'm sure the All-Father will make the right decision."

Odin closed his one seeing eye. The other, an empty black socket, stared into realms unknown by gods or man.

"I would willingly sacrifice the warmth of the sun and the light of the moon, but I will not part with Freyja. She is the sun and moon of Asgard," he finally said.

Loki looked like he was about to vomit, and he now voiced his opinion. As he was considered the wiliest of the gods, his words carried equal weight. He was not that bothered about light or warmth—he could live quite happily without both—but most of all, he despised Freyja, whom he had never managed to seduce into bed.

"Let's not be hasty, Father. The man looks strong, but the old nag looks on its last legs. Even if he worked day and night, he could never finish the task in that time, but he may give us a good start. We can't lose."

There was much shouting again until Odin spoke once more. "Loki has made a good point so I will leave it to Freyja to decide."

Freyja, to everyone's surprise, sided with Loki.

"For the good of Asgard, I say we give the stranger the job. Even half a wall is better than no wall at all."

Loki beamed, as well he might: this was a good deal for him whichever way you looked at it, and best of all, he had gotten out of having to do any work, as usual.

The stranger was brought in and told his offer had been accepted. He was invited to feast with the gods. For a man his size—like all mortals, he was very small compared to any of the gods—he ate and drank a prodigious amount, almost as much as Thor. But the gods were generous with their fare. They respected a man with a good thirst and appetite.

The gods rose early the next day, eager to see how the man would cope with the impossible task on top of what must be a horrible hangover. To their surprise, the stranger was already at work. He'd gotten up at the crack of dawn and led the old nag up the mountain where the gods quarried their stone. Unbelievably, the knackered old horse had managed to haul the huge rocks back down to Asgard. The stranger was already beginning to lay the foundations.

Some of the gods were troubled enough by this unusual behavior to visit Loki, who was not pleased to be woken so early.

"The man is clearly using magic of sorts." Loki yawned. "All the better for us. Even with the most powerful magic, he'll never get the wall finished in time, and we'll be able to finish off what he started. Believe me, I know about magic."

The gods were satisfied with Loki's reply. If there was one person who knew about sorcery, even the darkest kind, it was Loki. They returned to their homes to eat hearty breakfasts.

Loki, though apparently unperturbed, found he could not go back to sleep, and he kicked Sigyn out of bed to make him something to eat. He realized he was going to have to keep an eye on the mysterious stranger and take steps to hinder his rapid progress; otherwise, it would mean losing face in front of the Asgardians and worst of all, facing ,his father's wrath.

By the end of the month, the builder, with the aid of his old nag, had laid all the foundations for a massive wall encircling the whole of Asgard.

Loki now spent all of his days inspecting the wall hoping to find a crack, a bad join, or something out of plumb. But every stone had been laid to perfection. He found that even using his prodigious strength, he could not shift one stone to sabotage the stranger's efforts, so immaculately had they been cut and aligned. He could not use magic against the builder. If noticed, it would make Odin an oath-breaker for tricking the stranger. Loki's hands were effectively tied. He took to futilely cursing and kicking the rapidly growing wall in frustration every time he passed it.

Every night, the stranger would feast in the Great Hall while the horse hardly seemed to eat at all. He would join in any merry making but refused to be drawn out on how he was managing to build the wall at such a fantastic rate.

Winter ended, and spring arrived. The muddy and slippery road to the quarry started to dry out. The wall was half-finished. There was not the slightest gap between any of the stones. You could not even put a hair between the joins. Now the stranger was building apace. His movements were agile, but at the same time he never misplaced a blow from his hammer and chisel. The rocks he cut and placed were huge, and even a god would have found them difficult to move.

Odin and some of the other gods were watching the man's progress from a hilltop.

"He builds very fast," Balder observed unnecessarily

"No shit, Sherlock," Loki said.

"Who is Sherlock?" asked Balder with a puzzled look.

Odin gave Loki a warning look.

Loki waved his hand as if shooing away an annoying fly. "Nobody, a slip of the tongue," he said dismissively.

"Anyway, whoever or whatever he is, he's obviously not a man at all. At this rate, he could even have the wall finished before winter," Balder said.

"Maybe a giant in disguise," mused Loki.

"If only Thor was here," tall Honir said.

"Well, he isn't," grumbled Odin. "He's off thumping trolls, as usual when he gets bored. Besides, we made an oath, and as gods we cannot break an oath."

Freyja was looking very pale.

"Maybe we can break the oath without losing honor," mused Loki.

Freyja turned her beautiful dark eyes towards him. They had grown large and full of hope. His cock tingled as if she were about to place it in her mouth. Now Loki knew for a certainty that if he rescued Freyja from her predicament she would reward him with her cunt.

"And how do you propose to do that?" Hermod asked scornfully. He had not failed to notice the exchange of looks between Freyja and Loki and it had ignited a flame of jealous rivalry. Most of the male gods and quite a few of the females wanted to bed Freyja.

"I will think on it," Loki said and stalked off before he could be interrogated further.

The gods were muttering amongst themselves about it not being the first time Loki's council had gotten them into a mess, conveniently forgetting the times he had gotten them out of one.

They quieted when Odin spoke up. "It was indeed Loki's words that swayed us in this matter. He will pay for it with his life, and it will be a very painful death."

This didn't seem to lift Freyja's spirits at all.

Word got to Loki of his impending doom. It was nearing winter now, and the wall looked like it would be finished in a matter of days. It was time to do something drastic. Loki did not like the idea of Odin's threat of a painful death. Odin had a very vivid imagination when it came to inflicting pain.

They could never manage to pry out the stranger's name, but they did know the name of his horse, as he often called to it when it was time to be harnessed to the immense cart, which could hold over two dozen of the colossal stones.

Loki sincerely regretted thinking of the horse as an old nag; it was clearly one of the strongest horses ever born. Its name was Svadilfari, and despite its scrawny frame, it was very well endowed—very, very well, in fact. Loki gulped when he looked at the monstrous thing dangling between its legs. But a plan was a plan.

The builder stepped out of the dilapidated shed he had been given to sleep in. He stretched and grinned to himself as he greeted the morning. The sun was just rising, and its rays sparkled off the mountainous frost-covered flint wall as if it were embedded with diamonds. It only needed a few dozen more stones, and it would be finished. He took a deep gulp of the icy air, which was as refreshing as a mountain stream. It was going to be a good day.

He called out for Svadilfari and waited for the tell-tale sound of its hooves. Svadilfari was always glad to greet its master in the mornings as the man always carried a treat for it in his deep pockets. Today he had two red apples he had taken from the Great Hall under the reproachful eyes of Freyja. He took a large, crunching bite out of one of them, rejoicing in the thought that he would be between the squirming goddess's legs by nightfall—whether she was willing or not.

There was still no sign of his horse, so he whistled and called out again. His voice boomed off the hills and forests surrounding Asgard.

In the distance, he heard the welcome sound of his steed's whinnying. He smiled in anticipation, for he loved Svadilfari. The gods would, no doubt, have been astounded to see the stranger smile, because he always wore such a dour expression when in their company. But it was not one horse but two that came galloping towards him.

The man rubbed his eyes, but his eyes had not deceived him. It was, indeed, Svadilfari galloping towards him, followed by a beautiful chestnut mare.

The man had no need to be told it was a mare; because of the obvious state of his stallion's excitement. They both drew near, him their breaths like great plumes of steam. Svadilfari seemed undecided about staying with his master as the mare suddenly turned around and headed back into the forest. The man called to his steed once more and produced the apple. Svadilfari's loyalty to its master nearly won out, but a neigh from the disappearing mare seemed to make up its mind for it. It turned on its heels and raced off back to the mare.

The builder watched the disappearing rump of his stallion in disbelief. Svadilfari had never once disobeyed him. Now, in his moment of triumph, it had abandoned him for a wanton filly. Fate was fickle.

The gods were standing on a part of the completed wall and jeering at the builder, who had spent most of the day dragging the cart down from the mountain with just one of the huge stones upon it and was now struggling to get it off the cart and over to the wall. It would be night by the time he could even get around to cutting it. And once it had been cut he had the daunting job of pulling the stone single-handedly by winch to the top of the wall.

"I think your horse must be getting more than his fair share of oats. Do you think he'll be back by the spring?" shouted down Honir.

"You should have stuck with your horse and had a threesome. It's the only cunt you're likely to be getting now," jeered Balder.

The man could take no more. His face grew redder and redder until it was as crimson as the setting sun. Then he exploded. Literally. He revealed his true self. His body grew to its proper size of over fifty feet, for he was, in fact, a mountain giant.

"You have cheated me!" he roared at the gods.

The gods climbed down from the wall. Odin stood in the gateway with his arms folded, calmly facing the irate giant.

"No one has cheated you. It is you who have cheated us. Do you think we would have let you near Asgard if we had known you were a giant?"

"You are liars and cheats, and now you will pay," the giant said, picking up a huge rock in each hand and approaching the gateway, banging the rocks together menacingly.

"I think not," Odin said.

The gods parted, and the giant saw a hugely muscled god with flaming-red hair and beard. The god was whirling a great hammer in one hand. He aimed it at the giant's head and let go.

The giant watched it whirling towards him at incredible speed. It was the last thing he ever saw. The hammer hit him square in the forehead, and he was dead before he hit the ground with a reverberating thud. Thor had returned that morning.

The gods celebrated deep into the night. The only absentee was Loki, who was not seen for several months. When he did return, he was walking rather strangely, as if he had a bad case of hemorrhoids. Following Loki, and constantly nuzzling him as if he were its mother, was a foal. But it was no ordinary foal; it had eight legs. Loki gave it to Odin. It was called Sleipnir and would grow to be the fastest horse in the world.

None of the god's mentioned its parentage in front of Loki, and it would take a very brave Asgardian, indeed, to allude to it twice.

Loki spent several weeks recuperating in Freyja's bed. When Sigyn found out, he decided to have a hasty vacation in Ultima Thule.

CHAPTER FOURTEEN

MERLIN

The Pale Lady was haphazardly wandering in the garden in the vague direction of the lake, picking a fruit here and there. She had decided on an early-morning dip to refresh herself and wash off Thoric's dried seed, which covered the inside of her thighs.

A tall, hooded and black-cloaked figure stood at the side of the lake with his back towards her, staring out over the lake. His whole demeanor suggested a person in deep thought or peaceful contemplation.

He turned as she approached. It was impossible to make out any of the man's features, just two red pinpoints of light that passed for eyes.

After breakfasting and his morning ablutions, Thoric decided it was a good morning to test himself against the samurai.

He went to the appointed room and waited. He did not have to wait long. The warrior appeared in all his fierce samurai karuta armor. He was a very impressive and terrifying sight.

They went though the usual bowing ritual. Then they stepped on the training mat which Thoric had learned was called a tatami. All sparring had to cease the moment one of the combatants stepped off the tatami. Given the very limited amount of space, it was ideal for learning how to fight at close-quarters without ceding valuable space to move in.

They always started their sessions using staffs and then would progress to blunted swords. The samurai always used a traditional single-edged and curved katana, while Thoric had been presented by the Pale Lady with a blunted version of his own long-sword, Excalibur, exactly the same weight, balance, and reach without its razor edges and "fuller" to drain off the blood. The Vikings called these middle grooves "blood gutters," but Thoric had learned from the local village smith that they did not have much to do with draining blood; they simply made the blade lighter.

Fighting with a sword, especially, the samurai way had proven to be much more difficult than Thoric had imagined. It was simply because the samurai moved so fast and elegantly that Thoric thought he would simply imitate the warrior's movements and pick it up as he went along. Fighting as a Viking required speed and brute strength. Now he was learning about balance and breath control. They spent hours simply working on foot movement. The samurai only spoke to reprimand him, which was often. Thoric had spent many hours trying to learn Japanese, but despite all the books at his disposal and the efforts of the Pale Lady, he had still gotten no further than a few sentences.

One day, the samurai stripped himself of his armor and faced Thoric in a simple white robe tied with a black belt. Thoric did the same, selecting a robe that fit him and a thick black belt from one of the pegs that lined the room. The samurai looked at him furiously and shouted what Thoric thought could only be profanities. He ripped the black belt from around Thoric's waist, stormed over to the belt rack, and threw a white belt at Thoric's feet.

"Pick it up, dog," the samurai said. These words, Thoric did understand. "Dog" was what the samurai always called him.

"Yes, master" were the other words Thoric knew by heart. He picked up the belt as humbly as possible. His face was flushed with barely contained anger. The samurai had never uttered one word of encouragement to Thoric and would beat him with his staff at every opportunity. Thoric's body was a mass of bruises, each one a testimony to a mistake he had made. Not for the first time, he dreamed of hacking off the samurai's head with his axe, but he knew that there would only ever be one winner in that contest. At first, he had taken out this frustration in their unarmed combat lessons by launching unnecessarily violent attacks on his mentor, which had only led to worse beatings.

Now he had learned to repress any anger he felt, or even frustration. He fought coldly, with his brain, and found that the color of his belt was gradually changed by the master.

Finally the day came when the samurai bade Thoric kneel. Then he did an astonishing thing. He knelt in front of Thoric, bowed before his student for the first time, and presented him with a black belt.

It was the proudest moment of Thoric's life since he had been chosen for his first raid. That might have been months or years ago. There was no way of telling how time passed in the Pale Lady's castle, or in fact, the whole of Ultima Thule

"What are you doing here, Merlin? asked the Pale Lady. "On your last visit, you said you would never return."

She remembered their parting. It had been on less than amicable terms. During all his stay she had been plagued by strange dreams of having sex in the strangest positions and places. She would awaken every morning with the bed-sheets saturated with her juices. She had been sure that her night visitor had been Merlin, but when she had confronted him about it, he had been very offended and taken his leave. It did not seem strange to the Pale Lady that the nightly erotic dreams went with him.

One of the things that always annoyed Loki about humans, immortal or not, was their constant questioning. No one who knew the real Loki hardly ever had the temerity to question him or his motives, even gods.

The other thing that annoyed him was the rule that Odin had imposed upon the gods who had the skill to reach Ultima Thule—who were very few, anyway—which, was that they were not allowed to take their proper form. Loki would have loved to see the haughty Pale Lady shit herself and crawl at his feet, which was the normal reaction the man race had. It did make him smile, though, when they referred to him as the devil or evil incarnate, as if they actually knew what evil was.

The hooded figure spoke in the faraway voice that she had only ever heard in her worst nightmares.

"I lied," Merlin said. "All magician's lie. I thought you knew that, Eve."

"Don't call me that name. I don't like it. You know that."

"Nevertheless, it's your name, even though you may have forgotten it, or maybe you prefer Guinevere?"

"Will you stop, please." The Pale Lady had put her hands to her ears. "Why don't you just leave me alone? You drag the past around with you like a rotting corpse."

"Well, then let's return to the present. How is young Thoric coming along? Do you really think *he* is the one to keep you safe?"

The Pale Lady hid her surprise well. She did not know how Merlin had come to know about Thoric, but she supposed he had spies all over Ultima Thule.

"He killed the dragon, and the Lady of the Lake thought him worthy of Excalibur," she said.

Now it was Loki's turn to hide his surprise and annoyance. He had come specifically to take back the sword. It was his own weapon. It had been forged for him in secret by the greatest of the dwarf smiths, Brokkr, who had also forged his brother's lethal hammer, Mjolnir.

Excalibur was not meant to be handled by mortal men. He had only once allowed it—with disastrous results. The Lady of the Lake had specific instructions to kill any man who might try to lay claim to it.

Thoric was proving to be a thorn in Loki's side. Not only had he spurned his love after he'd allowed him to spill his seed inside him, but he'd killed his favorite pet, the Great Worm, and now this!

"The Lady of the Lake was meant to guard it, not give it to the first primitive human who happened to be strolling past," Loki said through gritted teeth.

"If I remember, you said that when you embedded it in stone to make sure no man could have it. The sword has a mind of its own. If it wanted to be with you, it would. Why don't you ask Thoric for it?" The Pale Lady smiled sweetly at him.

Loki knew his powers were limited here, and Thoric, with Excalibur in his hands might very well kill him. He would use other methods to obtain Excalibur and exact vengeance.

"If it has chosen him, so be it. Just make sure he uses it wisely." With that, he walked fully clothed into the lake.

The Pale Lady watched as the water enveloped Merlin until he had disappeared altogether in its murky depth. Relieved, she turned back to the castle. She had a sudden urge to have Thoric in her arms again. The encounter with Merlin had left her chilled to the bone.

Once underwater and out of sight, Loki assumed the form of a giant carp. He swam about leisurely, thinking while the fish part of him kept a beady eye out for predators. There was a particularly nasty old pike that inhabited these waters.

The fish seemed to reach some kind of resolution and darted towards a shadowy figure at the bottom of the lake. Loki circled around the Lady of the Lake, viewing her coldly through the large eyes of the carp. She could have been mistaken for a centuries-old abandoned statue, covered as she was with weeds and mud, but for her large eyes, the color of the lake, which continually followed the carp's every move. After circling her a few times, the carp gave her a mighty slap on the face with its giant fin, which toppled her over, and then it swam away.

A great carp leaped out of the lake in a majestic arc, its scales shimmering in the morning sun like a thousand gems. As it reached the peak of its arc, the scales and fins fell away, and a dark raven with crimson eyes took to the sky.

Thoric had noticed that one or more of the Pale Lady's ravens always seemed to be following him wherever his wanderings took him in the labyrinthine castle. Was she spying on him? He didn't think she'd do that. It was probably for his own safety to make sure he didn't get lost. Thoric decided it was best not to mention it to her. After all, she was only being thoughtful.

It was on one of these many scoutings around the castle, where rooms seemed to appear and disappear overnight, that he came across a vast and dusty old hall lined with tattered, ancient flags and worm-eaten shields depicting all kinds of long-forgotten coats of arms. At its center was a massive round oak table with equally large high-backed chairs, all exactly the same size and color as if they had all been cut from the same giant oak.

Thoric's father had once told him that you could tell the age of a tree by counting its growth rings when cut. The great, round table seemed to have been cut from the heartwood itself because the rings were clearly visible but Thoric gave up after the first hundred or so as they were too compact. He only knew it must have been a very great age when it was felled.

His father had also, more than once, visited Danelaw, and he had told Thoric many tales of the legendary island. One was of a great king that had ruled in the west of that island. He was said to have had a round table and a legendary castle. His father had told him the name once, but Thoric couldn't remember it. He knew that it had something to do with coming, and with that, his thoughts turned to his Asgerd. All thoughts of the round table and its knights were quickly forgotten as he hastened to the Pale Lady's chambers.

The raven, after experimentally pecking at the table, flew after him.

It was some days later, after his usual workout with the samurai and a bath in the lake, that Thoric went to the Pale Lady's chambers and found her washing between her legs with a linen cloth.

"I thought you were going for a walk, darling?" the Pale Lady said. Then she noticed Thoric's state of arousal. "Not again. That's a record even for you, Thoric!"

Thoric frowned in puzzlement. "What do you mean, and why are you washing your cunt?"

The Pale Lady's raven suddenly cackled in alarm and flew out the window.

The Pale Lady watched its receding shape and quickly gathered her thoughts.

"Sorry, my darling, I must have been having a wet dream about you. Come to bed."

Thoric did not need much persuading ...

CHAPTER FIFTEEN

THOR AND LOKI'S RIVALRY

Odin held up his hand. Both of his sons were talking over one another, and it was giving him a headache. "This constant bickering between you two has to stop. It's affecting Valhalla, but most of all, it's annoying me. Now, one at a time. Thor, you first. You look the most annoyed."

"He always looks like that," Loki said.

"I said Thor first!" Odin roared.

"Loki is once again interfering with Ultima Thule. He's been fucking the Pale Lady, who was promised to Thoric!"

"You know you would be, too," said Loki, "if you could shapeshift your way into Ultima Thule. As it is, you can only watch. Tell me, my brother, did you have a good wank?"

Thor's usually red face reddened even more.

"Listen to him, Father. He's even gloating about it!"

"Is this true, Loki? I thought you had gotten over the Pale Lady," Odin said.

"I still have a lingering crush. No harm done; she thought it was Thoric. Now she probably thinks he's started to fuck like a man at last."

"Thoric is my namesake, and he's proved himself worthy of the Pale Lady. Now Loki is abusing his woman!" thundered Thor.

"The way she was groaning with pleasure, she seemed to enjoy the abuse," Loki said, and he spread his hands in placation. "But if it makes you happy, Thor, I promise not to fuck her again while Thoric lives."

Odin nodded. "Sounds fair to me, Thor. What say you?"

"You better hope he lives a long life, Loki. I'm keeping an eye on you," Thor said, and the he stomped away.

"Dear me, brother, turning into a voyeur at your time of life," Loki called after him.

Thor gave him the finger without turning around.

The Pale Lady had always been very regular with her cycle. But a whole moon had turned, and there was still no sign of blood. At one time, she would have rejoiced at such a turn of events. Now she felt as if she were in mourning, for she was positive in her heart of hearts that she was carrying Merlin's child and not Thoric's.

Merlin had given her a host of strange, different-colored pills and instructions on how to use them when she desired to be with a man but did not want his child. After the deaths of the men she truly loved, she had remained in a kind of solitary confinement of her own choosing, for she blamed herself for their pointless deaths.

She had been content to remain in the wondrous castle, protected from the world by Merlin's pet. But Thoric had come into her life as promised by the ravens. Everything had changed but somehow stayed the same, as if she were a piece in a game played by gods.

Unknown to Merlin, the Pale Lady had her own way of disposing of unwanted offspring. Many centuries of experimenting with the herbs in her garden, and under the directions of her faithful cook, she had developed her own powerful concoction. But she had to wait for another full moon, and she needed to be alone. Where to send Thoric in the meantime? It had to be somewhere that even Merlin would not dare tread.

Thoric's fighting practices had changed drastically. Instead of the samurai, he now had two new teachers, who called themselves Chinese. They both had the same elegantly slanted eyes of the samurai, but they were very different. One was young, and one appeared to be extremely ancient. These men gave their names, which was a relief to Thoric, and the younger one was amenable to chatting, although the ancient one was so aloof he made the samurai seem positively friendly. Also, time stood still, if there was such a thing as time in Ultima Thule, when he practiced with them. He was not sure if he had spent hours, days, or even weeks practicing and eating with them, but when he emerged from the dojo, things were exactly the same as when he had entered. Only he had and his skills had changed

When he had asked the Pale Lady about this, she had shrugged and said it was the way of the castle. In a way, he was glad he could spend so much time in the grueling exercises as Asgerd no longer wanted to share her bed with him and seemed preoccupied with something she did not want to share.

His father had told him to expect such moments.

"Women will have their times when they want to be alone. I have learned over the years with your mother to respect those times. Their bodies hold the secret of life, and it's a heavy burden to carry, one that we men, poor, simple creatures that we are, will never fathom. It's best to leave them be. You will learn that when your time comes."

Thoric remembered these words every time he managed to meet with Asgerd. It was enough that she told him she loved him, and looking into her eyes he knew without a doubt her words were true.

His practice sessions were clearly divided into two parts. The first session was with the younger man, whose name was Ip Man, and he taught a fighting style he called Wing Chun. He was extremely amiable and chatty, and Thoric became devoted to him.

The session with Ip Man was followed by a small meal, which mainly consisted of fish and something Ip Man told him was called rice. At first, Thoric had found the white grains tasteless and bland, but now he found he enjoyed them as much as his lessons with Ip. After the meal, they would indulge in a practice Ip called meditation, a practice that Thoric found incredibly difficult as it involved remaining perfectly still. Staying still was not something he was good at, but he persevered, even if, most of the time, it was to please Ip.

The next session was with the ancient, whose looks belied his ability, which he considered superior to that of anyone in the world, or any worlds, for that matter. He sneered at the techniques of karate and the samurai's deadly swordsmanship, but he reserved his utmost scorn for Ip Man, whom he considered his inferior in every respect.

His name was Paì Mei, and he was master of Bak Mei, which he told Thoric was the greatest form of kung fu and was also known as the Eagle's Claw. Thoric had great respect for eagles, so he was a keen student. But nothing was ever good enough for Paì Mei. Thoric secretly desired to thrash Paì Mei, but the more he learned the more he realized that it was probably an impossible task, even if he used Excalibur.

Paì Mei's hair and long beard were a perfect white. He was extremely fastidious in his appearance. He kept his hair in a neat bun and his long beard neatly trimmed. His long robes were as perfectly white and immaculate as his hair.

For the first weeks—if they were weeks, or even months— he gave Thoric thankless and meaningless tasks, like carrying buckets of water from the lake up the numberless stairs of the castle and then emptying them from one of the turrets, or cleaning and scrubbing the immaculately clean dojo over and over again. But the most demeaning task was washing Paì Mei's robes, which he always managed to find some fault with, no matter how spotless Thoric got them. It was the most demeaning task you could give a Viking male, apart from asking them to wipe someone's arse. If Thoric dared to answer back or complain, Paì Mei would beat him mercilessly, and Thoric found he had no defense against these attacks. Paì Mei was so fast and, at the same time so elusive, that Thoric would find himself punching thin air. Paì Mei seemed to find this extremely amusing and would beat him all over again.

After a time, though, Thoric progressed to what Paì Mei called the "Three Inch Punch." It consisted of hitting a thick block of wood from three inches in a fruitless attempt to break it. Thoric would hit the wood until his fists bled and he could not move his fingers, and then Paì Mei would make him hit it all over again, Thoric had to bite his tongue to stop himself from crying out from the excruciating pain. He knew the sadistic Paì Mei would only enjoy it and probably use it as an excuse to beat him once again

When Thoric returned from these sessions his fists would be a bloody mess. The Pale Lady would merely tut; she had seen too many wounded men in her life to feel much sympathy, but she would gently wash his mashed hands with a mixture of herbs and warm water and then bind them with clean linen cloths soaked in wine. The cooling and soothing effect on his hands temporarily relieved the pain and raised his spirits, though he knew it would all begin afresh the next day.

"Why do you continue to do it, Thoric? Are you too proud to admit being defeated by a block of wood?" she asked.

"It's not the wood; it's him. He will gloat if I give up, I just know it, and he will send me back to carrying his stupid buckets again. At least with Ip, I can see the results of everything he teaches, and he always explains everything. He even apologizes when he hurts me!"

"Stay with Ip then. You don't need to take these lessons and punishment from this Paì Mei. He sounds awful!"

"Huh, there is nothing that would satisfy Paì Mei more. Besides, for some reason, Ip respects Paì Mei, although Paì Mei hates him. Sometimes I feel like telling Ip what Paì Mei says about him behind his back, but I'm not a tittle-tattle, and if I did, I would lose Ip's respect as surely as I would if I gave up."

"You say it's impossible to break this block of wood?"

"Even if I were hitting it a foot away with my axe, it might take me two or three blows."

"Why don't you challenge the old bastard, then?"

"What do you mean?"

"Tell him it's impossible and, if he's so great, challenge him to do it."

The thought of Paì Mei breaking his fist on the heavy wooden block somehow cheered Thoric.

"I will do it!" Thoric said.

He grabbed the Pale Lady by the waist and twirled her around laughing, and for the first time in many days, she laughed with him.

The next morning, he awoke happily, with Asgerd's arm draped lazily around his neck. He got up carefully so as not to disturb her and laid her arm on the pillow. She continued snoring quietly. He kissed her lightly on the forehead and went downstairs for some breakfast.

He arrived with a slight smile on his face as he greeted Ip Man. Ip took one look at him and grinned.

"Someone looks happy," Ip said in Chinese. He was a surprisingly good teacher, and not just of martial arts.

Wing Chun, Ip had explained to Thoric, was a form of Shaolin kung fu, and it was the Shaolin connection behind Paì Mei's hatred of Ip. The Shaolin considered teaching to be the highest art.

"Just looking forward to my lessons," Thoric replied in passable Chinese.

"I will try not to make them too strenuous. You have the look of a man who has had an active night. By the way, we have a treat for lunch today. I have finally managed to teach the cook how to make pork dumplings. And we have fried seaweed. Ever eaten seaweed, Thoric?"

"More times than you can possibly imagine," Thoric replied. "But first I want you to tell me the story of Paì Mei. You promised me you would one day. Today would be appropriate."

"Well, while I tell you the story, there is no reason that you should not practice."

Ip led Thoric over to the strange wooden dummy, or a mook jong, as Ip called it. Evidently, it had been made to his specifications by the dwarfs back when there was open communication with the castle, before the arrival of the Great Worm. Ip called it a wooden dummy, but it bore no resemblance to a man unless one had a very vivid imagination. It consisted of a thick trunk of wood with movable wooden branches meant to be arms and legs.

If one touched one branch, others would be set in motion, forcing the user to block the painful blows, but as soon as one was blocked another branch swung into motion forcing the assailment to move ever quicker until action and counter-action became a blur of constant parries and thrusts, from hands, arms, elbows, legs, knees, and feet. Even the head had to be used at times.

Thoric had grown to be well-versed in the use of Ip's contraption and often predicted the device's movement, but often as not, it would give him a nasty clout for being so presumptuous.

He fell into a steady rhythm of attack and parry as Ip began the story of Paì Mei.

"Paì Mei, 'White Eyebrows,' is one the legendary five elders who escaped the burning of the Shaolin Temple by Quing Dynasty forces. He then went on to help the White Lotus Clan lead a rebel army against the Quing. He then betrayed the rebels and the Shaolin monks to the Quing, killed a number of would-be assassins and avengers, and trained several teams of deadly assassins over the centuries.

"Paì Mei's kung fu is incredible. He can make himself as light as a feather, and a single strike from him can kill. The standard weak points of a human—throat, eyes, balls—are not only as strong as iron on Paì Mei, but they are weapons. He uses his inner thighs to break arms, his throat to break swords, and just his eyes to break hands. His *qi* is strong enough to deflect almost any attack. Apart from plucking out eyeballs for the slightest insult, Paì Mei's favorite method of dispatching an enemy is his Five Point Exploding Heart technique.

"It is said that many, many centuries ago in China, Paì Mei was traveling down a road when, a Shaolin monk crossed paths with him. Paì Mei gave a slight nod to the monk, who did not return it. Although the motives of the monk remain unknown, whether it was a deliberate insult or a misunderstanding (it was rumored afterward that the monk was, in fact, blind), Paì Mei tracked him down to the Shaolin Temple. He demanded that the head abbot kill himself as a means of retribution, but the abbot refused. Consequently, Paì Mei single-handedly massacred all sixty of the monks residing in the temple.

"Such are the legends surrounding Paì Mei," Ip Man said finishing his story.

"He sounds an absolute bastard!" Thoric said.

"He is not known as Paì Mei 'The Evil' for nothing," Ip said. "But there is no doubt that he is the greatest of the kung fu masters, evil or good. You can never hope to gain his respect, Thoric, but if you persevere he may deign to teach you some of his art. He has never, ever, to my knowledge, taught anyone the Five Point Exploding Heart technique, though. Perhaps you may be the lucky one."

Thoric did not consider himself to be lucky at all to be studying under the tutelage of Pai Mei. But it was with a renewed determination that he prepared for his coming lesson with him.

Thoric stood before the thick plank of wood. The first blow of the day was the hardest. His fists were usually healed over somewhat after the ministrations of the Pale Lady, but when he hit it for the first time of what would be hundreds of times over the session, all the newly formed scabs would be torn off and the raw, painful flesh revealed. The pain would shoot up his arms, and the plank would seem to double its thickness.

Pai Mei would be standing behind him with a scornful expression on his face to make sure that Thoric was striking it within finger-touching distance. He was waiting for Thoric to strike the first blow and stroking his beard, as was his habit.

No doubt the old man was gloating inside, Thoric thought, as he knew he had set the Viking an impossible task. Thoric stared at the hard-grained wood. He could sense Pai Mei's impatience.

"Perhaps you would like me to change it for a sheet of rice paper so you do not ruin your pretty little hands," Pai Mei said in the mocking tones he reserved for Thoric.

"It is a poor master who sets his apprentice a challenge he cannot complete himself," Thoric said, spinning around to face the inscrutable Chinaman. He knew he was causing grave offense to his master and teacher. He expected a beating there and then.

Instead, Pai Mei nonchalantly placed a finger on Thoric's shoulder which flung the now fully grown man several yards.

Thoric lay on the ground in disbelief and made to rise, but Paì Mei turned on him with sparks flying from his dark eyes.

"Do not rise. Lie there like the dog turd you are."

Paì Mei stood in front of the plank of wood and folded up one sleeve of his immaculate white robe. He measured out the small gap between the upright plank using his middle finger and curled his fingers into a fist. There was no sign of movement, only the sound of an almighty crack as the wood exploded into thousands of splinters. In the space where the plank had been, there was now Paì Mei's fist, which he slowly uncurled. Then he meticulously folded his sleeve back down and turned on his heels.

Without even sparing a glance at Thoric, he said, "Set up another plank, if you can even manage to do that with your delicate hands, which are only suitable for wiping a whore's cunt. Do not dare to appear before me again until you can break it with a single blow."

Thoric found himself wandering to the supply shed in a daze. He was still in a daze as he set the new plank up amongst the debris of the old one. He struck it all day until there was a puddle of blood beneath his feet. But when he walked away, he was satisfied that a crack had appeared in the plank.

The next day, he found that the cracked plank had been replaced with a fresh one. This time, he broke it with his first punch.

It had been some time since Thoric had visited his steed and friend, the crab. It clacked in delight when it saw Thoric and used its inner mandibles to stroke its master's face. Thoric walked with it to the lake and sat there talking to his friend in a mixture of the old Norse he had used when he had first arrived in Ultima Thule and the crab's favorite clacking noises. A raven with crimson eyes watched from a nearby tree.

Thoric took Excalibur down from the saddle. He kept it hidden in one of the saddle's secret compartments, wrapped in some old sack cloth, and tied with hemp.

The raven, as if this had been the moment it had been waiting for, let out a joyous shriek and flew from the tree like an arrow. It grabbed the package in its strong talons before Thoric had time to react, and then it took to the sky. The Viking could only stare in disbelief as the bird rose to the heavens with his treasure, squawking in delight and triumph.

Loki, in his raven form, could feel its small heart pounding with exertion and glee. He soared into the blue sky, cawing with pleasure and self-congratulation. The raven was so intent on making it to the forest before Thoric could regain his senses and unpack his bow and arrows that it did not notice the huge form approaching it from above until it blotted out the sun and it was too late.

The albatross thumped into it so hard that the raven all but lost consciousness. It dropped the sword and flew off to the forest. One of its wings was so badly damaged that it barely made it. The albatross landed in its usual clumsy manner. It might have been the height of elegance in flight, but it was as ungainly on the ground as a cow would be in the air. It waited for the rapidly approaching crab, which carried a worried-looking Thoric on its back.

Thoric jumped off the crab's back and alighted on the ground before the crab had even come to a halt. He ran up to the huge white bird, recognizing the albatross as the same sarcastic bird that had saved him from the eagles.

The albatross tilted its head to one side and regarded Thoric with its one good eye.

"You should take more care of your treasures, Thoric, son of Erin. There are always lots of thieves about, and not all of them in human guise."

With that, the albatross took a long, off-balance run to get its huge body back in the air.

"Thank you ... again," Thoric called after the bird as he bent to retrieve his sword, but it had already taken to the sky.

CHAPTER SIXTEEN

THE NUMB CITY

Loki was wandering around Asgard with his arm in a cloth sling. Just one look at his face warned the Aesir it would not be a good idea to approach him in his current foul mood. Even Thor, who was usually immune to other people's feelings, knew better than to disturb his brother's thoughts, although he missed their customary jests—cruel as they might be.

Loki's wife, Sigyn, made him his favorite dishes and poured him the best wine she could find. Nothing seemed to lift his depression. And even Sigyn, a giantess, who was renowned for her patience (you had to have tremendous patience to put up with Loki), had reached the point where she could not put up with his sulking anymore.

"Snap out of it, Loki, or I'm off!" she shouted at him from the end of the extremely long dining table.

Loki stared up mournfully from his untouched breakfast.

"Sigyn, I will tell you my problem as long as you promise not to reveal any of my secrets to the other Asgardians."

"You can't be serious, Loki! If I'd not learned how to keep my tongue, husband, half of Asgard would have strung you up by now. You know that, surely?"

Loki had to admit she was right, but she knew only the secrets he cared to share with her, and even those would have undoubtedly resulted in a torturous and long-drawn death. So, he told his wife everything about Ultima Thule, except for the Crab Prince and any sexual interactions with the Pale Lady. Instead, he told her about how he had hidden Excalibur and somehow Thoric, Thor's namesake, or, as Loki heavily hinted, probably one of Thor's mortal sons, had stolen it and was now probably plotting with the Pale Lady how to enter Asgard and murder Loki and all his family in their beds. Excalibur, was a sword capable of killing gods even when wielded by a mortal.

Sigyn was not usually sympathetic to Loki's problems, as they usually involved him being unfaithful to her in one way or another. But when a threat to her family was involved she could get serious. Very serious. Serious enough to actually seriously think about the mess Loki had got himself into. And so she came up with the solution.

The raven rapped furiously on the Pale Lady's window, waking her from a heavy and pleasant slumber. She turned to caress Thoric, but his place was already cold. He was always an early riser, whereas the Pale Lady was not a morning person.

"What the fuck do you want you stupid, stupid bird!" she yelled at it as she opened the window. Instead of heading straight for the feed tray, it hopped on her shoulder and cackled wildly in her ears. Then it flew off. She did not even have time to see its crimson eyes.

It had been nearly two months since the Pale Lady had bled, but she could still fit into her best robes, with no sign of the growth within her. That is what she now considered the fetus—not a living human being but a thing that had no right to be nesting in her womb, a thing planted there containing all the malice of Merlin.

Thoric stood alone on a parapet, looking north towards Storm Point and the Sea of Peril. The Pale Lady joined him soundlessly and also looked to the rugged northern skyline. She laid her head on his shoulder.

"You miss your home," she said quietly. It was a statement, not a question—an undeniable truth. Thoric did not know why he missed his homeland—the, only people he had ever loved there were his mother and father, and his mother was long dead, and his father would want nothing more for him than what he now had—but for some reason, he did.

He never told the Pale Lady of this sadness in his heart, as he was never more happy than when he was with her, but somehow she'd guessed. He should have known he could hide his heart from anyone but her.

Thoric told her about the misgivings in his heart and, the strange restfulness and melancholy he had been feeling of late.

"I think you need to travel for a while. Maybe it is adventure you crave, Thoric. You're a Viking, after all. You have a restless spirit."

Thoric mulled this over. Her words rang true, but he was loath to leave her. What if he could not find his way back?

As if reading his mind, the Pale Lady continued. "I have a solution that might temporarily serve us both. The ruler of the city of μούδιασμα has sent me word of rumors concerning a dark power rising in the Valley of Wishing. It troubles me. Perhaps you would do me the great favor of going to the city and consulting with the ruler. He can tell you his news personally, and you can give him your own impressions. You'd be my personal envoy."

Thoric had read in the books of forgotten knights that this was when the knight would bow and say something gracious, like, "It would be my great honor, milady," or something along those lines. But Thoric would have felt ridiculous. However, the idea of discovering more of the strange land and, at the same time, doing something worthwhile for his Asgerd thrilled him.

"No doubt, there will be many perils," he said.

"Many, I'm sure," the Pale Lady said, noticing the gleam of excitement in Thoric's eyes. "Enough to satisfy the bloodlust of any Viking."

She watched in quiet satisfaction as Thoric went off to prepare himself. Then a fleeting thought furrowed her brow for an instant. This really was too easy. She had been waiting for the news of Merlin's departure, and the raven's plan was a good one, but it now seemed all too pat. Something told her to be wary.

Thoric went to the part of the stables that now housed his giant crab. He carried a great sack of weapons with him, including Excalibur, his axe, and some more exotic ones that Ip Man had taught him to use.

What he saw filled him with consternation. The crab lay dead. Its giant shell was covered with some sort of fungus and emitted a putrid stink that filled even that vast stall. Thoric let out a cry of dismay and ran to the remains of his faithful friend. He lay his head on its pitted shell and wept.

In his head, he could hear the crab's joyous clacking, which had greeted him not more than a few weeks ago.

Through his deep groans of grief, he realized that the clacking was not just in his head. He spun around, and there was his friend, though now even more enormous than ever.

In his hurry to saddle the crab and be on his way, he had forgotten the Crab Prince's conversation with him about how the crabs grew to be so large.

The prince had explained it as being akin to a wealthy man-at-arms who grew increasingly fat as he aged and became more indolent. This meant that every year or so, he had to have a new suit of arms forged to accommodate his ever-increasing girth. But being of a generous nature, instead of having it smelted back down to create the new armor, he would give it to one of his many comrades whom it fit.

The crabs basically did the same, donating their shells to a smaller crab. For a while, the now-naked larger crab, if it could not find a discarded shell for itself, would remain soft-shelled until its new shell hardened.

This is what had happened to his old friend, who now stood before him with a magnificent new shell of red and orange, clacking its now-even-more-gargantuan pincers in delight and, Thoric could not help thinking, also with a touch of vanity, just as a man might proudly show off his new suit of armor.

Thoric had to make quite a few adjustments to the saddle to accommodate the crab's increased girth, but he managed it in the end. The crab seemed to be just as excited about the journey as Thoric, and it clacked merrily while Thoric loaded it up. Finally, after various struggles, Thoric was satisfied. The crab now resembled some sort of mobile fortress rather than any living creature. It was time for Thoric to take his farewell of Asgerd.

All the gods of Asgard had noticed the remarkable change in Loki. He went about the city, singing, making jokes with everyone he met, and generally spreading joy. At night, he celebrated in drunken orgies with his brother Thor and for a change, he gave no one a taste of his barbed tongue.

It all seemed to coincide with his return from the mysterious trip he had made some days ago. Loki had still been cackling to himself when he had arrived back in Asgard.

In fact, he had been laughing so much he'd forgotten to change into his normal form and had nearly been dealt an almighty, fatal blow by Heimdall the Gatekeeper, as no one, man or beast, could cross the rainbow bridge, Bifröst, into Asgard without Odin's blessing.

It was said that Heimdall's hearing was so acute that he could literally 'hear' a feather drop before it hit the ground. Luckily for Loki, Heimdall was powerful enough to see through his disguise. He asked Loki why he was so merry. Loki was too cunning to tell him the truth and said only that he had seduced a fair human maiden with his bird song. This, Heimdall did believe, as it was, in his opinion, Loki's nature to sow his seed by stealth and guile rather than noble wooing.

Loki had explained to the other gods that he had taken a much-needed vacation and now his arm, which had been causing him a great deal of pain, was thoroughly mended, along with his spirits.

Only Odin, out of all the gods, did not seem to share in the general merriment surrounding Loki, and he expressed neither any joy at his son's sudden recuperation nor, for that matter, any surprise.

CHAPTER SEVENTEEN

THE PLAIN OF FLYING DREAMS

Thoric felt truly happy on his journey. Asgerd, had been absolutely right, he decided, and he didn't know why he'd ever doubted it. He should have known. The Pale Lady was wise beyond measure. Now that they were apart, his love for her was rekindled, and he looked forward to carrying out the mission she had entrusted him with and returning to her open arms—and even more to her open legs.

On the second day, they came across a goat, and for the first time in a long while, he feasted on roasted meat sprinkled with some fresh herbs. It was delicious, although, at first, his stomach was upset with the rich fare. By the next day, though, it was settled and he had a good breakfast of the freshly cooked meat while the crab clacked happily as it picked at the raw remains.

He lay on his back and was greeted by a sight that sent shivers up his back. There were hundreds of bizarrely shaped birds flying overhead, but when they grew nearer upon closer examination he could see they were flying horses, not birds. Each one had a man or woman mounted on its back. The riders sat rigidly as if in a trance.

He knew then that he was on the Plain of Flying Dreams. According to what he had read, each of the people was asleep in lands far beyond Ultima Thule, and when they awoke, they would think that Ultima Thule was just a dream. "Such was the way of men," one philosopher described, "that they can rarely tell the difference between their dreams and the reality that lies under their noses."

There was a clear road leading to μούδιασμα, but Thoric decided to make a slight detour. On the map the Pale Lady had given him was marked a place that was held as sacred. It was called the Tomb of Longsleep.

By his calculations, they wouldn't have to stray off the road for more than a couple of miles. He took out the strange and wondrous device that the Pale Lady had given him. She called it a "spy-glass" and said it had been a gift of Merlin's. Thoric was not surprised that the wizard had been involved, for it did contain very powerful magic, but Thoric was nothing if not pragmatic. Though he usually shied away from magic, the "spy-glass" was very useful. It consisted of a small tube that, when you pulled on both ends, elongated itself to thrice its length, each part fitting neatly into the other. When you put the smaller end to one's eyes and pointed the larger end in any direction, it brought objects in the distance close to hand—close enough to touch. And many times, Thoric had tried to do just that, but it was impossible. The objects remained just as far away and stubbornly refused to be touched.

Thoric peered through the spy-glass in the general direction he believed the tomb to lie in. He made out a huge forest of what appeared to be giant red-and-white-spotted mushrooms and there, at the center was a vast edifice that appeared to be nothing more than a giant, long box. Thoric had no doubt it was the tomb.

He steered the crab away from the road and towards the forest. The crab clacked in annoyance; it obviously thought the road a better idea, but Thoric ignored it. He was also disobeying the Pale Lady, who had warned him not to stray from the road, but he was curious. He hadn't been out of the castle for what seemed like centuries, and for all he knew, in that timeless place, it may well have been.

As they got nearer to the blurred line of the forest, it did resolve itself, unbelievable as it was, to be a grove of giant, red-spotted mushrooms. Thoric, at first, had not trusted the spy-glass and thought some of the magic had gone amiss, but everything he had seen through the magical tube revealed itself to be true. And at its heart was the giant tomb.

Thoric got off the crab and walked around the huge stone monolith. It was, indeed, a sarcophagus of some kind as it had a lid. But it would need a giant of incredible strength to lift it. Thoric was pretty sure that if the lid was removed, it would reveal the remains of a giant's skeleton. It fitted in with the general conclusion he had reached regarding Ultima Thule, that the land had once been solely inhabited by giants, or perhaps gods, which sort of amounted to the same thing in Thoric's book. Thor, Thoric thought, if faced with the inaccessible tomb, would no doubt have smashed it apart with his great hammer, Mjölnir, and damn the consequences. But Thoric was content to view its grand, if plain, magnificence.

The whole glade was covered in dusty old cobwebs, which looked a hundred years old. As with everything else surrounding the tomb, the webs were enormous. Thoric shuddered as he pictured the monsters that must have sewn them—he hated spiders and had a keen dread of them, which amused his father, who was constantly collecting them and putting them down the back of Thoric's jerkin.

He noted the place was swarming with the docile rabbits so common in Ultima Thule. But these rabbits were even fatter and sleepier than any Thoric had previously encountered. They all seemed to be wandering around in a drunken haze. They reminded him of Vikings that had over indulged in henbane and were suffering from the after-effects of the drug. It did not matter to Thoric either way. He quickly dispatched a brace, skinned them, built a fire, and proceeded to boil them. He threw the raw remains to the crab, who clacked happily and proceeded to devour them with obvious relish.

Thoric flavored the rabbit with some dried herbs and also spent some time scavenging for some root vegetables, but there didn't seem to be any to be found. His eyes fell upon a little circle of smaller specimens of the red-and-white-spotted mushrooms that were about the size of his hand. He picked a few and sniffed them. They had what Thoric could only describe as an iron-like smell, which he knew was a good sign. Things that smelled of iron could only be good for you. The Vikings believed that meat or vegetables that smelled of iron made you stronger. But there was also an underlying disagreeable smell of cat's piss. He went back to his fire and bubbling stew and laid the mushrooms on the ground. The crab clacked in alarm when it saw the mushrooms. It clearly disapproved of them.

Thoric shooed the crab away with some annoyed clacks.

"I'm sorry you don't like mushrooms, old friend, but you have to admit our tastes in food are wildly different. I like my meat cooked, and you enjoy it raw. It's the same with fish, and you hate vegetables, but I like them, and they're good for men."

Thoric stopped his pontification. He could see his friend looked hurt, if a crab could have feelings. Thoric had come to believe the crab possessed many.

"Don't worry, old friend, I intend to try a small piece of the mushrooms before I eat them. Just like my mother taught me." He was never sure if the crab understood him, but he was sure the crab understood the sentiment behind his words. Thoric gave the crab some reassuring clacks and popped a small piece of mushroom in his mouth. The crab somehow deflated, turned its back, and proceeded to search for grubs and worms in the soil.

After about half an hour, Thoric had experienced no unwanted sensations. They weren't poisonous, so he chopped up the remaining mushrooms and chucked them in a pot. Five minutes later, he removed the pot from the fire. His mother had always warned him about overcooking vegetables, and he considered her words more valuable than gold.

Once the stew had cooled enough to eat, he took out his wooden spoon and hastily devoured it, and he found it delicious. After a while, a pleasant, sleepy sensation enveloped him, and trusting his crab to guard him, or at least to alert him to any dangers, he put his back against a warm boulder and fell into a deep sleep.

Thoric dreamed the strangest and longest dream he had ever had. He dreamed of giant pink spiders, each one nearly the size of the crab. They attacked him while he was still sleeping, dreaming this strange dream of a dream within a dream.

For some reason, his limbs felt extraordinarily stiff and unyielding, as if he had stayed in the same position for far too long. He stripped to wash in a nearby brook and experienced another shock: his whole body was a mass of purple and dark green bruises and livid scarlet welts as if some manic artist had used him as a human palette. What's more, scattered everywhere were the hacked-off limbs of one or more of the pink spiders. The legs did not look half so impressive as they had when attached to their owners. The legs were covered in fine, glossy pink hairs that gave the spiders their distinct coloring.

As Thoric marched around half-naked to relieve the cramp in his thighs and calf muscles, a ghastly stink assaulted his nostrils. He was hardly surprised when he came across the corpse of the spider. The only thing that did astonish him was the state of the dead spider's body. This was no fresh kill. It must have been deceased for over a week. Even stranger, it bore the unmistakable cuts of Excalibur. Only that enchanted sword left such clean cuts. It was as if the mutual parts of the whole had never been united at all and had always been disconnected.

Thoric put the pieces of the puzzle together finally and made a hasty exit from the vicinity of the aptly named 'Tomb of Longsleep'.

Thoric finally finished telling the crab what had happened, which made little difference to the crab, who had watched the whole scene unfold without being hindered by the consumption of mushrooms. It could have led Thoric to the spot where he had first been ambushed by the spiders while he was hallucinating.

The crab had slaughtered over a dozen of the repugnant creatures. The remaining spider had followed them back to the camp, and there it had tried to jump on Thoric. It had learned quickly that it was best to avoid the crab. But Thoric, unlike the usual prey the spiders feasted on after they were rendered somnambulant by the mushrooms, had reacted instinctively from his many years of oriental training and, in a blur of speed, had drawn his sword from its scabbard on his back and sliced the spider into pieces before it had time to even realize it was dead.

Thoric had then sat down by the fire, vomited, and gone to sleep. The crab had waited patiently for three moons until the effects of the mushrooms had disappeared and a somewhat dazed Thoric had woken up properly. He had promptly vomited again.

The crab contented itself with regaining the road and clacking sympathetically wherever it deemed it was necessary throughout Thoric's explanation of why the tomb had been given the name of Longsleep.

Thoric had surmised that the tomb was never originally called Longsleep, as it had no markings and was only relevant to the people who had made it, but had acquired the name because of the mushrooms. Then the spiders had moved in, sensing easy prey whenever any animal ate the fungi, and the tomb's name had acquired an even more sinister connotation.

The crab clacked its agreement, but it wasn't quite sure if the human understood. They could be quite stupid at times ...

Thoric was making haste now because, no doubt, the Pale Lady would have been informed that he had still not arrived at the city of μούδιασμα. It was a strange name for a city, Thoric thought: "Numbness". When he'd asked Asgerd, she had said he should consult the city's ruler for an explanation of its provenance.

It wasn't until the next morning that he saw the spires of what appeared to be a massive city emitting an eerie green glow. He looked through the spy-glass and saw that it was as magnificent as described in the books in the Pale Lady's library. The sight dazzled him in the morning light as it seemed to be made entirely of green emeralds. The city itself was surrounded by a murky green moat and protected by high marble walls. There seemed to be no end of riches in Ultima Thule, enough to satisfy even the most voracious of Viking kings.

Thoric felt, not for the first time, a slight feeling of shame for his people. He could imagine them running riot here, laying waste to everything they could not carry, leaving in their wake death, misery, and raped women and children. Was that all the Viking race would be remembered for—savagery?

As he drew near the city, he saw there was some sort of welcoming committee emerging from the city's gates. It was a ragbag of different creatures, many that Thoric had only heard about in legend.

There were seneschals, ogres, gnomes, trolls, witches, warlocks, elves, and even dark-elves. In their vanguard was someone, or something, wearing an ornate crown, the king and ruler of μούδιασμα—a huge bloated toad. It was all too much for Thoric, who felt both humbled and horrified at the same time. The crab made its discomfort obvious by clacking its huge front pincers. The crowd fell back in obvious fear, so Thoric dismounted and approached the king and his minions on foot.

"We have heard you would be visiting us," the Toad King said. His voice, far from being the croak that Thoric expected from one of his species, was deep and melodious, almost songlike. The strange entourage escorted Thoric into the city of Numbness.

The king, who hopped alongside Thoric as gracefully as a regal toad could, told him that they had prepared quarters for him and his crab in the palace. Thoric thanked him. He had now gotten over the initial shock of talking to a toad. He'd talked to albatrosses, so there didn't seem to be too much difference. At least the toad wasn't sarcastic.

A feast was given in Thoric's honor, accompanied by the best ales and wines the city could offer: soup of barley and venison; salads of sweetgrass, spinach, and grapes sprinkled with crushed walnuts; snails in honey and garlic (a platter of which Thoric ordered to be taken to the crab); freshly caught trout baked in clay; and then pigeon pie and a course of meats roasted in their own juices, served on thick trenchers of day-old bread. This was all rounded off by sweetbreads and baked apples, fragrant with red wine and cinnamon, and lemon cakes frosted in sugar, accompanied by a very thick, sweet white wine.

They were entertained by various mummers, who enacted stories that appeared to be well known to the audience but made little sense to Thoric.

Thoric partook of every course, each seeming to be better than the last. He found he had a fearsome appetite, no doubt induced by the forced fast after what he now called the "magic mushroom episode."

He sat in the place of honor at the high table on the right side of the king. Thoric noticed that his host very rarely ate from any of the dishes, which had obviously been prepared for human tastes, but instead would occasionally lean over and take the lid off a jar of large blue-bottle flies, which he expertly caught with a flick of his long, sinuous tongue.

After the long meal, Thoric was invited to the king's private chambers. If Thoric had expected the room to be strange or eccentric, he was sorely disappointed

It was easily the most normal room he had ever been in. Compared to the rooms in the Pale Lady's castle, it was practically rustic. The walls were bare of hangings, and there was one low table clearly meant for the toad and some cushions—that was all.

Thoric handed over the letters of presentation from the Pale Lady and the private letter that was meant for the king's eyes only. The toad, Thoric noticed for the first time, had almost human hands with fingers and thumbs. He even wore a huge emerald ring, which glittered as he flitted through the papers. He handed them back to Thoric after the perfunctory examination.

"All is perfectly in order, as I expected, my dear Thoric," he said. He then picked up the private letter and spent a lot more time perusing this missive. He re-read it several times, and at certain passages, his eyes bulged, and a toad's bulging eyes are not a pleasant sight.

"Is anything wrong, my lord?" Thoric asked.

"No, no, nothing to concern yourself with, Thoric. The Pale Lady merely inquires about the dangers threatening my city, which are manifold, but you may be of help to us with one or two of your ... skills. I should tell you that the citizens of this city are unused to violence and have no skills in battle and military matters. I think first we should consult my wizard. He can reveal things in more ways than one."

The Toad King hopped over to one of the walls and tapped some sort of code on it. A hidden panel swung open, and there stood the wizard.

In every appearance, this wizard bore a distinct semblance to Merlin. Thoric bit his tongue and restrained himself from burying an axe in his head.

"Greetings, Thoric, son of Erin. Welcome to μούδιασμα."

The voice from under the hood did have the same sepulchral tones and burning red dots for eyes as Merlin, but as Thoric had never seen the wizard's face he was not sure it warranted the man's death. Also, the Toad King might take it amiss.

The Toad King handed the wizard the Pale Lady's letter. The wizard, being a man of letters, read it very quickly. He glanced up at Thoric once during his reading, as if regarding the Viking as a curious type of insect. When he finished, he put the letter somewhere in his voluminous sleeves.

"It seems I am entrusted with showing you some of the troubles afflicting μούδιασμα, but to do that, first you should know some of its history. Look out of the window, Thoric, and tell me what you see," the wizard said.

Thoric stared down at the streets. After the eclectic mix of personages that had greeted him at the gates, Thoric had forgotten that there might be human men and women in the city. In fact, when he looked down, he saw that the majority of the inhabitants were, indeed, human.

They all shared something in common: they moved in a trance-like state, their eyes fixed, clouded over. It was as if they were all sleepwalking through the day's routine, locked in a never-ending dream. They all bowed mechanically to one another as they passed each other by.

Thoric turned away from the window.

"They look like they are all asleep. What's the matter with them? Why are they this way?"

The wizard bade Thoric sit down and then proceeded to tell him the fabulous story of the city of μούδιασμα, or the Numb City, as he called it. Once, it had been a bustling, thriving city at the center of all trade in Ultima Thule, but its ruler had become greedy for even more power and riches. He assembled a powerful army and proceeded to declare war on the faerie folk. He craved their gold and intricately made jewelry above all else.

The faerie queen was very annoyed at the impudence of the mortal king and sent out a formidable army of faeries, elves, and dark elves. There was a great slaughter, the city of μούδιασμα fell, and its wicked king was killed. But after walking through the streets strewn with the slain, hearing only the crying of women and children lamenting the deaths of their husbands, brothers, and fathers, the queen felt great remorse. She was not an evil queen and had a kind heart, if faeries could be said to have hearts, so she brought all the dead back to life except for the evil king.

She wiped the memories of all the people of the city by enchanting the waters of a great waterfall so they would not remember the terrible war, and she set the wise Toad King to rule over them. Thus, the people of the city lived happily in a perpetual state of forgetfulness.

"It is this state of forgetfulness that is at stake. Every week, the inhabitants go to the Waterfall of Old Songs and fill their jars with its waters. They mix it with water from the city's

well and maintain their forgetfulness. And now a singular
warrior stands guard before the waterfall and will not let any
pass. If they dare, he slaughters them without compunction.
We have to keep them from waking up completely."

"Why?" Thoric asked. "Would it be such a bad thing?"

"Yes! said the Toad King. "It would be a very bad thing.
Many of the older men and women who survived the war still
hold grievances and vengeance in their hearts. If they awoke
fully, they would pass it to the next generation, and it would
not be long before the old hostilities were revived. They were
spared only so they could raise a new generation free of
prejudice. When the time is right, the humans will be
awakened, have no fear, but this is not the time. This warrior
seems to want to revive the war."

"One warrior against a whole city. What's the matter with
you?" Thoric said.

"There lies the problem," the magician said. "He seems
impervious to all magic, and no one can defeat him in mortal
combat. But the Pale Lady tells us you're no ordinary warrior
and that you possess an enchanted sword. She is sure you can
defeat this enemy, and we will reward you accordingly."

"What reward?" Thoric asked, more interested now.

"The reward will be a bottle of the sacred water. A small
sip, and you will be temporarily relieved of all your troubles
and heartaches. Believe me, there are many who would
willingly pay with their lives for such a thing."

Thoric thought it over.

"Done," he said.

CHAPTER EIGHTEEN

THE WATERFALL OF OLD SONGS

The Pale Lady was happy with the news her raven had brought. At last, Thoric had arrived at the city. She had little doubt that he could defeat the nameless warrior. Then, with the prize he had won, he could return to her castle and her now empty womb.

She had removed all traces of the creature that Merlin had sewn within her, and the aftereffects of the poison had been less severe than her previous experiences—it was as if the fetus had somehow known that it was cursed. However, she had not let herself see it just in case her fears were unfounded. When she next lay with Thoric, she would make sure it was his baby. She had woven a shield, which she had placed above her bed to ward off unwanted dreams and doppelgangers. Merlin, despite his cunning, would not impregnate her that easily again.

The Pale Lady was looking forward to tasting the water from the Waterfall of Old Songs. A small sip had helped her forget many of her woes. It would also put pay to Thoric's wanderlust and longing for his stupid homeland.

Thoric had arrived at the waterfall with a small retinue, who were to be the official witnesses of the combat. He had not been allowed to bring the crab. Evidently, according to the city's bylaws, any duel between two combatants had to be on foot and could only take place between them, with no interference from any of the witnesses. Thoric had been forced to admit to the Toad King he did not have that much control over his steed and could not guarantee the crab's impartiality.

There was another reason the crab was not present, but Thoric had no knowledge of what had befallen his friend and companion, and if he had the magician would have been a head shorter.

That very morning, after Thoric had clacked reassuringly to the crab that he would soon be back and had left him with a bucket of juicy snails, the magician had crept into the stables and filled the bucket of snails with pure, undiluted water from the Waterfall of Old Songs. Now the crab was wandering around as if it were intoxicated and its brains were completely addled. All it could remember was that it had come from a beach and somehow it should return to others of its kind. With no other thought, it set off in what it believed was the general direction.

In fact, the magician had placed in its memory a completely different beach, and now the crab was headed for Cramp Beach, which was on the other side of the Sea of Peril, whose waves kissed the western walls of μούδιασμα. The magician was quite sure that it would not be long before it was devoured by the monstrous octopuses that plagued the sea's depths.

The entourage followed the course of the river that sprang from the falls. Thoric asked the Toad King why they simply did not draw the water from the river. He realized as soon as he asked the question that it was a stupid one.

"To drink from the river is deadly, as many have found out to their cost. Only the waters in the pool at the bottom of the fall are safe to drink and then only if they are very diluted. Otherwise, you would forget yourself entirely."

As soon as Thoric got near enough to hear the crashing splash of the waterfall, he could make out the warrior guarding it. It was no ordinary man. He was nearly twice the size of Thoric and wielded a great net and trident. Nevertheless, Thoric felt no fear at all. Master Paì Mei had taught him to suppress all physical emotion and use it to his advantage when fighting.

Thoric did not even give the giant time to utter his challenge. He ran at him full pelt, skipping lightly over the net in one bound. Drawing Excalibur from the sheath on his back, he cut the trident in half, and with the back sweep, he cut the man in half. There was a look of disbelief in the man's eyes. His mouth was still open as the top half of his body fell to the ground. The legs bizarrely remained standing even as a fountain of blood erupted from the severed torso.

The witnesses, who had not even had time to draw breath, hastily recorded the incident on their scrolls or drew a series of pictures for those who could not read. Many just vomited.

The Toad King bade everyone return to the city and gather the men and women so they could celebrate Thoric's victory and fill their jars.

"Thoric, the city of μούδιασμα is forever indebted to you. You are, indeed, a great warrior, and your fame shall spread throughout my kingdom," the king said. He bowed to Thoric, who bowed back, but the Viking seemed very distracted and was looking pensively at the waterfall.

The magician turned to the king.

"I will remain with Thoric a while. I think he can now hear the music."

"Do not linger too long lest you both lose your wits," the king warned.

"Don't worry, I'll look after Thoric. We'll return shortly if it so pleases his majesty."

The king nodded and followed the others back to the city.

The magician came and stood beside Thoric, who could, indeed, hear something in the waterfall. It sounded like a far-off lullaby, something his mother might have sung to him as a child.

"What do you hear, Thoric, son of Erin?" the magician asked.

"For a moment, I thought I could hear my mother's voice," Thoric said.

"Come closer to the pool. You'll hear better."

Thoric stood on the bank of the swirling waters and gazed into its dark depths. He was sure he could now hear his mother's voice. It seemed to be coming from the bottom of the pool.

"Yes, I am sure I can hear her now. I remember my cradle, and she was gently rocking it and singing this song. The words ... if I could only hear the words properly ..."

The magician glanced over his shoulder to make sure that the entourage was now far away.

"Then why don't you join her, Thoric," he said. And without further ado, he pushed Thoric into the raging waters.

Thoric struggled for a while, but the weight of his weapons dragged him down. Down to the very bottom. All that remained was a corpse, neatly parted in two, and a black cloak, which lay crumpled by the bank. Far off in the sky, a large raven crowed triumphantly as it flew towards the mountains, Excalibur held tightly in its talons.

CHAPTER NINETEEN

THE MAN WITH NO NAME

The man who clambered out of the river miles downstream, where it forked, could neither remember his name nor from whence he came. He was covered in river weed and mud.

He lay down on his back as exhaustion overtook him and stared up at the night sky. The heavens were as unfamiliar to him as his own mind. But he could still somehow remember that the twinkling white lights were called stars and the twin giant yellow plates were called moons. He reached out to touch them. They were so close, but also so far.

Winged shapes with people sitting on their backs flitted occasionally across the moons' faces. Some faced forward, and some backward. The winged horses carried what he knew to be men like him, women and children. Some were in pairs, and some alone. They all shared one thing in common: they sat straight in their saddles and never moved. The man thought it would be nice to ride one of those horses, but they never landed and never deviated from their path towards the shadowy line of mountains to the north.

He fell asleep where he lay, too tired to seek shelter or warmth. The truth was, he did not feel cold; in fact, he did not feel anything—he was just numb.

END OF BOOK ONE

COMING SOON:

ULTIMA THULE, BOOK TWO

THORIC THE ASSASSIN

CHAPTER ONE

THE THING IN THE SWAMP

It did not know its name. It only knew It had a presence. It had an ancient presence in this particular place, and now It had been disturbed. It had awoken once again.

The large, grizzled man at the bar had just ordered another tankard of ale when the terrified man approached him. The man coughed in a vain attempt to make his voice stronger.

"Are you the one they call Thoric?" he asked nervously to the giant's back.

The other drinkers backed away slowly. You never knew what sort of mood Thoric was in when he'd been drinking. He was nearly always sullen and filled with battle lust, but it only varied in degrees from his innate anger with human kind in general. This could usually be measured by the number of corpses he left in his wake.

The man was in luck. The warrior was not in a particularly belligerent mood. Thoric turned slowly and looked down at the trembling man.

"Some call me that. What do you want?" he said in a voice better suited to a bear. "I'm drinking."

"Perhaps you would like another one?"

The man had grown in confidence. His head still remained on his shoulders. A lot of bets were hastily changing hands behind his back.

Thoric drained his tankard and slammed it on the counter to be refilled.

"Now, tell me quickly. You're wasting my drinking time," Thoric said.

"To hire your services, if you please."

The man waited for some sort of blow to fall on his head, cringing slightly. There was no blow. He opened his eyes. Thoric was stroking his beard. The man did not know it, but he had happened to find Thoric at a very opportune moment. Thoric was low on funds, and a deadly mercenary low on funds tended to listen rather than kill on the spot.

Thoric beckoned the man to a nearby table. It was occupied, but the occupants magically disappeared as Thoric's hulking shadow fell over them.

"Tell me," Thoric said as he sat on a creaking chair.

He transfixed the man with frozen blue eyes that seemed to reflect the ice-laden barbaric land from which he was said to hail. The man knew that he should only speak the truth to this son of Nordic gods.

The man began his tale, and a stranger one, Thoric had not heard in his many years of wandering without direction ...

Other fiction books.

Nazi Lesbian Vampires - available at all major online bookstores and on my website: https://stephenhernandez.co.uk/

Reviews:
5 STAR!
"Take a short, 2 to 4 hr. Trip inside a different take on the Third Reich and it's insane bid to use the occult to take over the world."

***** (5 stars)

Gigi

WORTH A READ!
"Definitely worth a read! I'm sure there will be more amazing titles from this author to come."

***** (5 stars)

Kindle Customer

Inside the Madhouse - available at all major online bookstores and on my website: https://stephenhernandez.co.uk/

Reviews:
LOVE!
"I loved it!"

***** (5 stars)

Dee Crain

GREAT VARIETY!

"20 great stories, well worth a read!"

***** (5 stars)

Amazon Reader

Non-fiction books.

Learn to Speak Spanish - Without Even Trying! - available at all major online bookstores and on my website: https://stephenhernandez.co.uk/

GREAT VALUE FOR MONEY!

"Really helpful tips on how to learn to speak Spanish it is money very well spent."

***** (5 stars)

Kindle Customer

Learn to Speak German - Without Even Trying! - available at all major online bookstores and on my website: https://stephenhernandez.co.uk/

SUPER ADDITION!

" Learn to speak German is a super addition to this series of books from an author whose love of languages shines through in his writing. "

***** (5 stars)

Amazon Customer

Learn to Speak French - Without Even Trying! - available at all major online bookstores and on my website: https://stephenhernandez.co.uk/

Learn to Speak Italian - Without Even Trying! - available at all major online bookstores and on my website: https://stephenhernandez.co.uk/

Learn to Speak Portuguese - Without Even Trying! - available at all major online bookstores and on my website: https://stephenhernandez.co.uk/

ABOUT THE AUTHOR

Stephen Hernández was born in Bromley, England, (the only characteristic he shares with H.G. Wells and David Bowie but he always finds it worth mentioning anyway as a point of interest), but spent a lot of his childhood in Venezuela. He has lived and worked in South America for a large part of his life. At one time he ran a nightclub in one of the most dangerous cities in Venezuela; after surviving cancer, he concluded that surviving a terminal illness was far less dangerous than running a nightclub in Venezuela. He works as a translator and interpreter of Spanish, with a specialization in medicine. He now divides his time between England, Italy and South America. When he is not working, he likes to write.

https://stephenhernandez.co.uk/